Gates

Tor Moor

Torwarsh Uilliage

Esfearp

Gorm

Sulcar
Keep

Sippar

Place of Wisdom

Yle

Etsford

Es

Lormt

South Keep

Eyrie of Falconers

Cave of Volt

Verlaine

Karsten

Kars

Copyright 1977 by Barb Johnson

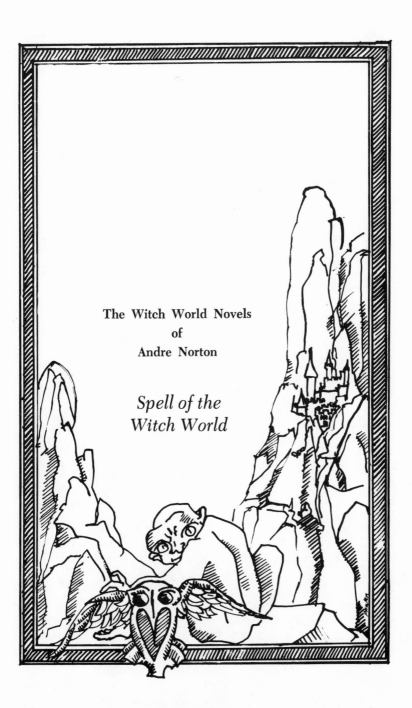

The Witch World Novels
of
Andre Norton

*Spell of the
Witch World*

**The Witch World Novels**
**of**
**Andre Norton**

*Witch World*
*Web of the Witch World*
*Three Against the Witch World*
*Warlock of the Witch World*
*Sorceress of the Witch World*
*Year of the Unicorn*
*Spell of the Witch World*

# Spell of the Witch World

ANDRE NORTON

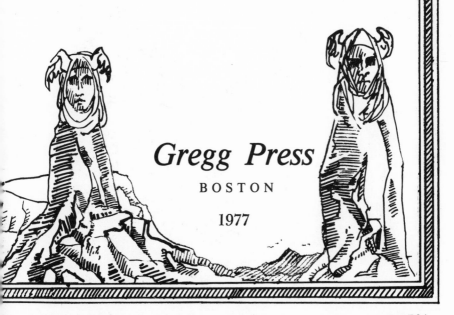

*Gregg Press*

BOSTON

1977

This edition published in 1977 by Gregg Press
A Division of G. K. Hall & Co.
by arrangement with DAW Books, Inc.
and with the cooperation of Andre Norton

Jacket and text art by Jack Gaughan
Frontmatter art by Alice Phalen
Endleave maps by Barbi Johnson

**Library of Congress Cataloging in Publication Data**

Norton, Andre.
Spell of the Witch World.

(The Witch World novels of Andre Norton)
Reprint of the ed. published by Daw Books, New York.
I.   Title.   II.   Series: Norton, Andre. The Witch
World novels of Andre Norton.
PZ3.N8187Sn5   [PS3527.0625]   813'.5'2   77-23206
ISBN 0-8398-2354-1

Manufactured in the United States of America

*Spell of the
Witch World*

# DRAGON SCALE SILVER

# 1

## *The Coming of the Far Strangers*

THE STORM had been high, battering the cliffs, breaking over the half reef which gave protection for anchoring the fishing boats. But the men of Wark had had warning (for none are so weather-wise as those who live by wind and wave and the changeful sea-luck). So no boats were lost, nor men either—save only that the smaller yawl of Omund was driven up on the beach so he must inspect it carefully.

Omund was not the only one upon the wave-pounded sands that morning, for sea storms, if they do not take wantonly from what little stores of goods a man may garner, sometimes give. Thus all of Wark who could keep to their feet and had keen eyes were down on the strand seeing what bounty might have been deposited at their very doorsteps.

Sometimes amber was found so, and that was a precious find. Once Deryk had come across two gold coins, very old, with signs on them Aufrica, the Wise Woman, said were of the Old Ones. So Deryk took them to the smithy straightaway and had them melted into a lump, thus removing any magic curse from good metal.

Always there was wood, and the kelp from which women could make dyes for winter wear, and shells, which the children treasured. Sometimes the wreck of ships, such as never anchored in the reef-guarded small-bay of Wark, nor which most of the people had ever seen the like of—nor would unless they traveled to Jurby port.

This time came the strangers. At first those on the beach thought the boat drifting in deep water was wreckage, and then there was a flutter of movement aboard. Yet there were no oars. When those on shore called and waved (though their voices might well be lost in the crying of the sea birds) there came no answer.

At last Kaleb of the Forge stripped and swam out, a rope about his middle. Then he waved vigorously to let them know there was life aboard and made fast the rope, so the men, pulling together, could bring in the boat.

In it lay two, though one leaned against the side, her salt-tangled hair about her wan face, her hands moving weakly as she tried to brush it from her eyes. The man lay quiet, a great wound upon one temple as if he had been felled in battle, so that they first thought him dead. But Aufrica, bustling forward, as became her calling of healer, pulled aside his sodden tunic and listened for the heartbeat, declaring that the sea, or ill fortune, had not taken him yet. Thus with the woman, who seemed in a daze, unhearing their questions, only brushing feebly at her hair and staring wide-eyed, he was taken to Aufrica's house.

So the strangers came on the storm edge to Wark. And thereafter they stayed, though they remained strangers. For the wound which had felled the man had in a manner changed him. At first he was like a little child and the woman fed and cared for him as if indeed he was one she had before carried at her breast.

Their clothing, sea-stained and stiff with salt, was not that of villagers, nor was the woman like any they knew. At first, Aufrica reported, she had not their tongue, but she learned it speedily. Then Aufrica, who had always been open, spoke less and less of those she sheltered. And when Gudytha, the headman's wife, and others asked questions, she was evasive, as if she harbored some secret which both awed and excited her.

The women of Wark spoke long and often to their goodmen, and at length Omund came to the house of Aufrica as Headman to ask the name and purpose of the strangers that he might send word to the Lord Gaillard in whose territory Wark lay. For this was in the Year of the Salamander, before the great war of the invaders, and High Hallack was at peace, with law within its borders, especially along the coast where the settlements dated from the early days.

The stranger man sat in the sun, his healed wound leaving a scar across his forehead. Except for that he was comely, dark of hair, with thin, well-cut features which were not those of the Dalesmen. He was slender of body, though tall, and Omund noted that his hands, which lay slackly on his knees, were not calloused as his own from oar and net, but rather those of a man who had not labored thus for a living.

He smiled at Omund with the open frankness of a child and there was that about him which made Omund smile back as he would at his own young son. And in that moment he thought that for all the tittle-tattle of the village wives and the talk over the wine-horns of the men, there was no harm in this poor stranger and he had come on a useless errand.

At that moment there was the opening of the door and he looked away from the smiling man to face the woman who had come out of the sea in his company. Straightaway something stirred deep in Omund's mind, though he was a simple man who found the events of each day enough to think on.

She was nigh as tall as he and, like the man, slender and dark of hair. Her face was thin to gauntness and there was certainly no trace of beauty, as Omund reckoned it, in her. But there was something else—

He had been to the great hall in Vestdale to be confirmed in his headship for Wark. There he had seen the Lord of the Dale and his Lady sitting in state, all power and authority. Yet when he faced the stranger woman, wearing a kirtle made from one of Aufrica's and badly fitting, too, with no gems on her fingers or at her throat, her hair braided but with no golden bells to dance lightly at the ends of those braids, he felt more awe than he had in the full splendor of Vestdale. It was her eyes, he afterward decided—nor could he have told the color of them, save that they were dark and seeming too large for the thinness of her face. Still in them—

Without thinking Omund took the seaman's knitted cap from his head and raised his hand palm out as he would to the Lady of Vestdale herself.

"Welcome in peace." Her voice was low, yet had in it a kind of controlled power, as if she could shout down the mountains behind them if she wished. She stood aside for him to enter.

Aufrica sat on a low stool by the fire. But she did not rise nor bid him welcome, leaving all to the stranger as if this was not now her own house, but rather she was visitor within its walls.

On the table was the hosting-horn filled with the good wine of hospitality. Beside it a platter of welcome cakes. And the strange woman held out her hand as was the custom, her fingers light and cool on his sunburned wrist. So she brought him to the table, taking the stool opposite from him across the board.

"My lord and I have much to thank you for, you and your people of Wark, Headman Omund," she said as he sipped the wine, suddenly grateful for such a familiar thing when all else seemed to take on strangeness. "You have given us both second life, which is a great gift indeed. And for which we are in your debt. Now—you wish some accounting of us—as is proper."

He had no chance to ask the questions he had formed in his mind; she was in command here even as a Dale lord would be. Nor did he resent that; it seemed right and proper.

"We come from overseas," she continued. "But there is ill doing there, the hounds of war cry. There came a time when we must choose between death and flight. And since no man, nor woman either, chooses death unless hope is fled, we took ship for a new land. There are the Sulcarmen who dwell in ports of their own along our coast, and through them we learned of this land. It was on a ship of theirs we took passage.

"But—" For the first time she hesitated, looked to her own long-fingered hands where they rested on the tabletop. "There was a storm," she continued as one who must put aside certain thoughts, "and the ship was sore beset. My lord was struck down by a falling mast as he was to come into the boat. By a great mercy—" here her fingers moved as if she made some sign, and Omund saw Aufrica stir, heard her draw a deep breath, "he fell to me. But there were no others reached us and we drifted until you found us.

"I speak frankly now with you, Headman. What gear we had was lost with the ship. We have naught now, nor any kin here. My lord mends, he learns from day to day as a child learns from birth, yet faster. Perhaps he will never regain all the storm took from him, but he shall be able to play a man's part in the world. As for me—ask of your Wise Woman—I have certain gifts which match hers, and those are at your service."

"But—would it not be better that you go to Vestdale—?"

She shook her head at Omund's suggestion.

"The sea brought us here, there was doubtless a purpose." Once more she signed upon the table and Omund's awe grew, for he knew now this was one like Aufrica, but greater, so it was well Aufrica did her handmaid's service. "We remain here."

Omund made no report to the Lord at Vestdale, and, since they had delivered the year's tax at Jurby, the Lord's men had no reason to visit Wark. At first the women were inclined to keep apart. But when the stranger tended Yelena in such a birth that all swore the babe would not come live from her body, yet it did and lived, and Yelena also (after the stranger had drawn certain runes on her belly and given her to drink of herbs) there was no more talk. Yet neither did the goodwives treat her with such friendly wise as they did Aufrica, for she was not of their blood nor kind, and they called her always Lady Almondia, just as they spoke with deference to her man Truan.

As she said, he mended, and when he was fully well went out with the fishers. Also he devised a new way of rigging nets which added to their catch. He, too, went to the smithy and there he worked with a lump

11

of metal he brought out of the hills until he had a
sword. This he practiced with as if against future need.

Often together the Lady and Truan went to the hills
in directions those of Wark never took. Oh, men had
half-wild sheep there which they kept for the shear-
ing. And there were deer, and other game to provide a
tasty change from fish. But there were also things of
the Old Ones.

For when the Dalesmen came up from the south
into this land it was not a barren world. Though the
Old Ones were few, for many of them had withdrawn,
no man knew where. Those who remained had little
traffic with the newcomers, keeping ever to the high
places, the wastelands, so that one saw them only by
chance.

Strange indeed were the Old Ones and not all of
one kind as the men of High Hallack. Some seemed
monstrous. Yet in the main they did not threaten man,
only continued to withdraw further.

However, they left behind them many places wherein they had once built their own strongholds, places
of power. And these, though well built, men shunned.
For there was about them a feeling that it was well
advised not to disturb their ancient silences, that if one
called too loudly or too arrogantly, one might be answered by that better not to face.

There were places also where remnants of powers
or influences still clung. Into these one could venture
and deal with such—if one was foolhardy and reckless.
If you gained, the saying went, your heart's desire from
such dealing, yet in the end the sum was dark and grim
and you were the worse instead of the better for it.

One such place stood in the hills above Wark and
the hunters, the herders kept afar from it. Nor did the
animals they trailed or tended ever stray in that direction. Yet it was not noted for evil as some places were,
but rather for a feeling of peace, so that those encroach-
ing upon it by chance were oddly shamed, as if they
disturbed the rest of something which should not be
so troubled.

There were low walls, no higher than a man's shoulder, and they enclosed a space, not square, nor rectangular, but a five-pointed star. In its centermost core was a star-shaped stone set as an altar.

Within the points of the star sand was spread, and those stretches of sand were different in hue. One was red, one blue, one silver, one green, and the last as gold as the dust of that metal. No wind ever seemed to blow within the walls, and the dust was always smoothly spread, as if it had not been disturbed since first it was shifted there.

Outside the star-point walls there was the remains of a garden which was a tangle of herbs. It was there that Aufrica went three or four times a summer to harvest those simples she used in her cures. After the coming of the strangers both went with her first, and then alone. But none spied to see what they did there.

It was from such a trip that Truan brought back the lump of metal he wrought into a sword. Later he brought back a second mass and fashioned a shirt of mail, so cunning his work that Kaleb and fishermen alike would watch, marvel at how deftly he drew out metal into threads or wire, formed them into interlocking rings. As he worked he always sang, though the words were not in their language, and he appeared to be in a dream from which he could not be easily roused.

While he labored the Lady Almondia sometimes came to watch, her long hands clasped one over the other tightly as if she willed herself to some hard action. Her eyes were sad, and she would leave with drooping head, as if she watched some fateful thing which had in it the seeds of abiding ill. Yet never did she speak, nor strive to halt his labors.

There came a night in the first of autumn when she arose before the moon was to be seen. She touched the shoulder of Aufrica who lay in her own bed place. While Truan slept they went forth from the house and took the trail up and up. The moon gave light as they reached the top, to show them the way as clear as if they carried lanterns.

So they went, the Lady Almondia first, and Aufrica after, and each carried a bundle in the crook of her arm, and in her free hand a wand of ash peeled white and silvered by moonlight.

They passed through the old garden and the Lady climbed the wall, her feet setting prints in the smooth sand which was silver. Aufrica, following, took care to step in the tracks the Lady left.

Together they came to the star altar. Opening her bundle Aufrica took out candles, finely fashioned of beeswax and scented with dried herbs. She set one of these on each point of the star. While the Lady unrolled the packet she carried and brought out a cup. It was roughly made of wood, as if it had been shaped by hands not accustomed to such a task. Which was the truth, for she herself had labored in secret to hollow it.

This she placed in the center of the star. Into it she shifted a little of the sand taken from each point, putting in a double handful of the silver. So the rude cup was half full.

She nodded then to Aufrica, for they had done all in silence, not breaking the brooding quiet. The Wise Woman threw around the cup full handfuls of a white powder, and when that was done the Lady Almondia spoke.

Thus calling upon a Name and a Power. And she was answered. Out of the night struck a bolt of white fire to ignite the powder. And that blaze flared so brilliantly Aufrica cried out, covering her eyes. However, the Lady Almondia stood steady, and now she chanted. As she chanted that blaze continued, though there was naught for it to feed upon. Over and over again she repeated certain words. At last she flung high both arms, and when she lowered them slowly to her sides again, the blaze died.

But where there had been a cup of rough wood, there was now a goblet shining, as if fine silver. The Lady took this and covered it quickly, holding it to her as if it were some treasure she valued with her life.

The candles had burned away, but they left no dripping of wax where they had stood; the stone was bare. The women turned and went. Aufrica glanced back as they climbed the wall. She was in time to see a small ruffling of the sand as if it moved under some invisible, unfelt wind, to wipe out the footprints they had left.

"It is done, and well done," the Lady spoke with a wearied voice. "There remains now only the end—"

"A lusty end—" Aufrica ventured.

"There will be two."

"But—"

"Yes, a double wish carries its own price. My lord shall have his son, who, as the stars have written will company him. Yet, there shall be another to guard."

"The price, Lady?"

"You know well the price, my good friend, my moon sister."

Aufrica shook her head. "No—"

"Yes, and yes! We have both cast the seeing runes. The time comes when one must go, the other be left. If the day of going comes a little sooner—for a good purpose—what matters that? My lord will have those to watch after him. Look not so, moon sister. You and I know that such partings are but doors opening, not closing—though the dull eyes of this world see very little. Rejoicing, not sorrow shall be our portion!"

Though she had always been so sober of mien and quiet, it did seem that the Lady Almondia thereupon put on lightsome airs she had not shown before. And there was a kind of beauty about her as she bore the cup back to the house.

There she filled it with a special wine of Aufrica's best. With it rim-full in her hand she went to the couch of her lord and laid her hand upon his forehead. He awoke easily and she laughed and spoke to him in her own tongue. Then he laughed also and drank of the cup halfway. She finished the rest and went to his eager arms and they lay together after the way of man and wife and were fulfilled while the moon sank and the first light of dawn grayed the sky.

Not long after it was seen that the Lady was bearing, and now the women of the village felt less in awe of her and they would speak freely, telling of this or that which was of aid to women in her condition. Always she thanked them softly, with good will, and they brought her small gifts, a length of fine wool for a wrapping band, things to eat which were proper for a breeding woman. She went no more to the hills but worked about the house, or sometimes sat silent, her eyes fixed upon the wall as if she saw there what others could not.

But Truan became more than ever a part of the village. He went with Omund to Jurby for the year's tax and trading venture, and when they returned Omund was high pleased, saying that the Lord had made an excellent bargain with the Sulcarmen so they reckoned more from this venture than for many years previous.

Winter came and people stirred not far from their homes, except at Yule eve when they had the Year's End Feast, the women tossing ivy, the men holly onto the fires to bring luck for the Year of the Sea Serpent now beginning.

Summer came after an early spring and there were babies in the village, Aufrica overseeing the birthing. The Lady Almondia no longer went out. And several of the goodwives began to watch her and shake their heads in private, for, though her body thickened, yet her face was very thin, her arms like wands for size, and she moved as one with a burden greater than she could bear. Yet she smiled at all and seemed content. Nor did her lord appear to notice any change in her.

Her time came with moonrise on just such a brilliant night as that when she and Aufrica had evoked whatever was within the star walls. Aufrica brought forth oils over which she said old spells, and upon the Lady's belly she wrote runes, and upon the palms of her hands, and upon her feet, and last of all on her forehead.

It was a long labor but it ended at last with the crying wails of not one babe but two. Side by side they lay on the bed place—a boy and a girl. The Lady, too weak to raise her head from the pillow, looked to Aufrica with a message in her eyes, so that the Wise Woman came quickly to her, in her hand the cup of silver.

16

In this she poured a small measure of pure water and held it so that the Lady could, with infinite labor, raise her right hand and set fingertip in it. With it she touched the girl babe who cried no longer, but lay looking about her with strange, almost knowing eyes, as if she could understand all that was happening.

"Elys," said the Lady Almondia.

By her stood the Lord Truan, a kind of horrified awareness in his face as if his season's long gentle acceptance of life was ended with bitter knowledge. But he reached also finger to water and touched the boy babe who was crying lustily and kicking as if he fought. And he said:

"Elyn."

Thus were they named, and they grew well. But within four days after their coming the Lady Almondia closed her eyes and did not wake again. So she went from Wark after her own fashion and when she was gone they discovered that indeed they were much the poorer. The Lord Truan let Aufrica and the women make her seemly, then he wrapped her in a woolen cloak and carried her in his arms into the hills. Men, looking upon his face, did not ask him where he went, or if they could aid him.

On the second day he returned alone. Nor did he ever mention the Lady again, but became a silent man, willing to give aid in any matter, but seldom speaking. He continued to live with Aufrica and he cared for the children with more attention than the village men were wont. But no man remarked on that, for he was no longer one they felt easy with—as if some of that which had always cloaked the Lady was now wrapped about him in turn.

# 2

# *Cup Spell*

THAT WAS THE BEGINNING of the tale, before it was mine. I learned it mostly from Aufrica, a little from my father, who was Truan, the Far Stranger. For I am Elys.

There was more that Aufrica told me concerning the Lady Almondia. Neither she nor my father were of High Hallack nor of the Dales blood. They came from Estcarp, though my father said nothing of their life there. And what my mother had told Aufrica was little.

Aufrica, being a Wise Woman, had the lore of herbs, knew charms, could make amulets, ease pain, bring children, had the powers of the woods and the hills. Though she never attempted the mastery of high sorcery, nor called upon the Great Names.

But my mother had been more, though she used what she knew sparingly. Aufrica believed she had set aside much of her power when she fled her native land with my father, the reason for that I was never to learn. But my mother was witch-born, sorceress trained, so Aufrica was like a newly schooled child in her presence. Yet there was some barrier so that she might not turn much of her past authority to use in High Hallack.

Only when she wished children had she invoked what she had once been able to call upon freely. And then she paid a high price—her own life.

"She cast the rune sticks," Aufrica told me. "On that table there, she cast them one day when your father was afar. In those she read her own future was short. Then she said that she must not leave her lord without what he longed for—a son to bear sword and shield after him.

"It was the nature of her kind that the bearing of children is not often known. For they put off much of the woman when they take on the cloak, put out their hand for the wand of power. They must break vows and that is a fell thing. But she was willing to do this for her lord."

"He has Elyn," I nodded. At that moment my brother was indeed with our father, down with the boats drawn out of winter seas to be worked upon against summer out-faring. "But there is also me—"

"Yes." Aufrica's hands were busy as she crushed dried herbs into a scented paste in the mortar she held between her knees. "She went to a place of the power to ask for a son, but also she spoke for a daughter. I think that she, also, wished one to take her place in the world. You are witch-born, Elys, though what I can teach you is very little beside what your mother knew. Yet all I have learned shall be yours."

A strange upraising indeed. For if Aufrica saw in me my mother's daughter, to be nurtured with the learning of old powers, my father saw a second son. I did not wear the kirtle and skirt of a village maid, but breeches and tunic like my brother's. This was to suit my father, as he was uneasy if I appeared before him otherwise.

Aufrica thought that was because as I grew older and taller and more of a woman I resembled my mother and that made him unhappy. So I kept to the likeness of Elyn and he was satisfied.

It was not only in apparel that my father wished me son rather than daughter. From the earliest years he taught me arms-play, matching Elyn and me. First we thrust and parried with small, mock swords made from driftwood. But as we grew older he beat out twin blades in the smithy. And I knew as much of the art of battle as any Dales squire.

However, he yielded to Aufrica, that I had my time with her. We quested into the hills for herbs, and for her to show me certain places of the Old Ones and relay to me the rituals and ceremonies which must be observed at phases of the moon should it be desired.

19

I saw the star-walled place where my mother had wrought her High Moon Magic, but that we never ventured in though we brought harvests from about the walls.

I had seen many times the cup my mother had brought from that final sorcery. Aufrica kept it among her most precious things, never touching it with her bare hands, but always with a square of green-blue stuff she valued highly. It was silver in color, that cup, but also other colors ran across its surface when it was turned this way or that.

"Dragon scales," Aufrica told me. "This is dragon scale silver. I had heard of it in old legends, but never did I see it before the dragon fire itself wrought this at the Lady's bidding. It is thing of very great power; guard it well."

"You speak as if it is mine—" I marveled at the cup, for it was a thing of such beauty as one might see only once in a lifetime.

"Yours it is when there is time and need. It is bound to you and to Elyn. But only you, being what you are, can make use of it." Nor did she say more then.

I have spoken of Aufrica who was very close to me, and of my father, who walked, talked, and lived as if a thin sheet of some invisible armor cut him away from the rest of mankind. But I have not spoken of Elyn.

We were born at one birth, yet we were not close copies of one another. Only in our faces and persons was that so. Our interests were never the same. He loved action, swordplay, and he chafed at the narrow life of Wark. He was reckless and often disciplined by my father for leading other boys into trouble or danger. And he used to stand outside at times, staring at the hills with such longing in his eyes that he seemed a hawk in chains.

I found my freedom inwardly, he wanted his outwardly. He had impatience for Aufrica's teachings. And as he grew he spoke more often of Jurby, of going there to take service with a Dales lord.

That my father would have had to let him go at last

we knew. But in the end war answered that for us. For in the Year of the Fire Troll the invaders came to High Hallack.

They were seaborne, and, when my father heard of their raids upon the coast keeps and towns, his mouth set hard. For it seemed that they were enemies long known to his own people. He put aside those moods of other-being when he walked apart and one night he spoke to us and Aufrica with the determination of a man who had decided upon a course and would not be turned from it.

He would go to the Lord of Vestdale and offer his sword—and more than his sword, for knowing this enemy of old, he had that to offer which could prepare resistance the better. Looking upon his face we knew that nothing we might say or do could turn him from this course.

Elyn then arose and said if my father would go, then he also as squire. And his determination was as set and stern—their faces alike, one to the other, in that moment as if one was the mirrored reflection of the other.

But my father won that battle of wills, saying that Elyn's duty was to me and to Aufrica for the present. But he swore a binding oath that he would send for Elyn later, so his authority held.

However, my father did not depart at once; rather, he wrought in the smithy day and night. But first he went into the hills with a pack pony. When he returned his animal was heavily laden with lumps of metal which might have once been worked and then congealed into these masses.

From these he wrought, Kaleb aiding him, two swords and two shirts of fine and supple chain mail. One of these he gave to Elyn, the other he brought to me. When he laid it down he spoke as one who would have his words heeded, to be remembered in days to come.

"I do not have the gift of foreseeing that she had" —seldom did he mention my mother, and then never by name—she might have been some great lady he

21

held in reverence and awe. "But I have dreamed, and of my dreams has come this—that there lies before you some venture in which you must go girt with more than your strong spirit and courage, my daughter. Though I have not treated you as a maid—yet—"

It seemed that words failed him. He stroked the mail shirt as if it were silk, nor did he look directly at me, but turned sharply and went before I could speak. And in the next dawn he took the hill path to Vestdale. Nor did we ever see him again.

The Year of the Fire Troll passed, and as yet we dwelt safe in our small clift pocket, we of Wark. But Omund made no year-end voyage to Jurby, for a small band of hard-used folk came over the hills to tell us Jurby had fallen to the enemy in a single night of red wrack and ravage. And that Vestdale Keep was now besieged.

The villagers met and tried to plan. They had always lived by the sea, yet it seemed now that the sea might be their bane and to flee inland meant safety. The younger men, and those without strong family ties, spoke to make a stand where we were. But others thought it better to abandon the village and return later if no invasion came nigh.

Tales of the refugees swung the day, for those hearing their accounts of the red ruin the raiders left urged retreat, and that decision won.

During all debate my brother listened but did not speak. I read in his face that he had made his own decision. So when we went back to the house I faced him and said:

"There comes a time when one can no longer keep sword in sheath. If you would go—go with our blessing of good fortune. You have served your time here; be sure we shall have safety on our side when we take to the hills, for who knows their secrets better than Aufrica and I?"

For a long moment he was silent and then he looked at me straightly.

"There is bred in me that which I must answer, for

22

a year I have been trapped here. Yet I was promise-bound."

I went to Aufrica's cupboard, and she, sitting on a stool by the fire and watching, said not a word. What I brought forth was the dragon cup of our heritage. When I set it on the table between us I let fall the wrapping and set my two hands boldly about the cool curve of its sides. So I held it for the space of a few breaths.

Then Aufrica arose in turn and brought from her stores a bottle of herb brew I had never seen her open before. She drew its stopper with her teeth, keeping both hands about it as if she feared she might drop or spill what she carried. Into the cup she poured a thick golden liquid, and a spicy odor filled the room, carrying with it the plentiful ripeness of a good harvest, the slumberous fullness of early autumn.

Halfway she filled the cup as I held it; then she drew back, leaving Elyn and me facing each other across it. I loosed my hold, reached out, catching his hands, drawing them to the smooth silver.

"Drink," I told him, "half of this, drink. For it is the cup we must share before we part."

Without question he raised it two-handed, and did not set it down again until he had swallowed half the potion. Then I took it in turn and finished what was left.

"While we are parted," I told him, "I shall read your fate in this. For while the silver remains clear as you now see it, then all is well. But if it clouds—"

He did not let me finish. "These are times of war, sister. No man walks safely forever."

"True. Yet sometimes ill can be turned to well."

Elyn made an impatient gesture. Never had he taken any interest in wise knowledge. It was as if he deemed such of little value. Still we had never brought this difference into words. Nor did we now.

Rather I put away the cup and worked with Aufrica preparing what he must take with him, covers to sleep warm in on the trail, food and drink, as well as a wallet of healing herbs. And, like my father, he went.

23

But those of Wark left also. Some of the younger
men followed my brother like an ill-drilled menial. For
he was, in spite of his youth, a leader amongst them
in his knowledge of arms. The rest of us barred the
doors of our houses, loaded our pack ponies, and took
to the hills.

That was an ill winter. We found refuge, first in an
inland village, until an alarm of raiders came—then farther inland in barren country. Until we lived in caves
and other rude shelters. Always came tales of farther
and farther invasion, more and more taking of High
Hallack.

Aufrica and I were much called upon for our knowledge of healing, not only of wounds when wanderers
from lost battles chanced upon us, but of the many
illnesses which come from hard living, hunger, and
even of hearts giving up hope. Since we faced dangers
which were more sharp and sudden, I wore the mail
my father had fashioned for me, knew sword-weight
at my belt. Just as I learned to use the bow for hunting, both for the pot and for those who would prey
on us for what sorry possessions we had left.

As it always is when there is no law in the land
and only war and more war, season after season, there
were those who had been born of our own kind and
now skulked as filthy scavengers, preying on all too
weak to defend themselves. I killed in those days and
knew no sorrow for it, for those I so slew were not
truly men.

One thing I kept ever by me was the cup, and
each morn I took it forth to look upon it. Never was
its brilliance dimmed, so I knew all was right with
Elyn.

Sometimes I tried to reach him by a dream bridge,
using a sleep potion. Yet all I bore back into wakeful-
ness was a confusion of half memories. At those times
I hungered for more than Aufrica could teach me, for
what my mother must once have had.

In our wanderings we came nigh now and then those
places of the Old Ones. From several we urged our
now small and stumbling band away. For what crept

like a foul fog from those was evil malevolence, wholly alien to our kind. Others were empty—as if what they had once cupped was long fled or had seeped away through the years. A few were welcoming, and to those Aufrica and I went, hoping to evoke something of what centered there. Yet we had not the proper training to take more with us when we left than a sense of peace and inner refreshment.

There were no longer named years for us, just the passing of seasons. In the third summer we found refuge at last. Some of our band had split away, choosing other roads. But our small remaining group, with Omund at its head (he was now much crippled with an aching ailment of the bones), his younger brothers, their wives, two daughters with children whose husbands had followed Elyn (for which they sometimes looked ill at me yet never spoke their feelings aloud), and three more households in which the men were elderly, remained together.

We found a way into a small upland dale which had never been settled or visited save by shepherds in season, or cattle drovers, who left huts where they had sheltered during the grazing months. There we stayed, our handful of sheep, our half-score of footsore ponies, glad to be at rest. And the people who had spent their lives combing a living from the sea turned with patient labor to win some sustenance from the hills.

In high places overlooking the two passes we kept guards. So different had life become that those guards were mainly women, armed with bows and with spears which had once been the harpoons of deep-sea fishermen. Well did we keep watch and ward, for we had seen several times what chanced in small settlements when those raving wolves of scavengers came down.

It was midsummer of our second year in that pocket of earth, and most of the others were at labor tending what grain and roots we had saved for this season's planting, that I was on hill watch and saw for the first time riders on that faint track which would bring them to the south pass. I raised my bared sword and with the sun flickering on its bright blade signaled the

25

alert down valley. I myself went by previously learned
ways to spy closer upon those who came. For by this
time we judged all strangers enemies.

As I lay upon a sunwarmed rock and watched, I
could see that they were little threat to us. For we
made up in will and preparedness enough to handle
these two.

They were plainly fighting men, but their mail was
rusted and gashed. One had been tied to his saddle
and drooped so he might have fallen to the ground
had it not been for those ties and the fact that his
comrade rode close beside him, leading his mount.
There were bloodied rags bound around the head and

the shoulder of the half-unconscious rider, and about the forearm of his companion.

That companion looked time and again to their back trail, as if he expected pursuers. He still wore a helm topped with a crest of a swooping hawk, though one wing of that was shorn away. And both had the ragged tatters of heraldic coats over their mail, though whatever device those had once displayed was so raveled as to be unreadable. Not that I was learned in the symbols of the noble Dale houses.

Both men had swords, now sheathed. And the helmed one a crossbow. But they had no field packs, and their mounts ambled at a footsore pace, as if nigh to floundering.

I inched a little back and got to my feet in the shadows, setting arrow to bow cord.

"Stand!"

My order must have seemed to come from empty air. The helmed man jerked his head. I could not see his face clearly because of the overhang of his headgear, but his hand was on sword hilt in swift, sure movement. Then he must have thought better of what might be useless defiance, for he did not draw.

"Stand forth yourself, lurker, steel to steel!" His voice was hoarse and low, but he bore himself as one ready to meet trouble as it came.

"Not so," I answered. "I have that which will pin death to you, bold man! Come out of your saddle and put your weapons from you."

He laughed then.

"Cut me down as you will, voice from the rocks. I put aside my blade for no man. If you want it—come and take it!"

Now he deliberately drew his weapon, held it at readiness. Even as he faced me so his comrade stirred and groaned, and the other urged his horse a little on, pushing between the wounded man and where he must believe I stood.

"Why do you come here?"

His constant glancing at his back trail remained in

my mind and I wondered if he led more trouble to us. Two such men we could handle—but more—

"We come no place." There was vast weariness in his voice. "We are hunted men as you can guess if you are not blind. Three days ago Haverdale stood rearguard at the Ford of Ingra. We are what is left of that force. We bought time as we promised, but how much—" He shrugged. "By your speech you are of the Dales, not the Hounds. I am Jervon, once Marshal of Horse—this is Pell, my lord's younger brother."

That bristling defiance seeped from him; the weariness lay like a heavy burden on him. And I knew—as if I had cast runes on it—that these men were no menace to my people, unless they drew after them what we could not handle.

So I came out of hiding. As I wore mail, he believed me a man, and I let him think it. But I brought them into the Dale and to the tending of Aufrica.

Those with Omund were first ready to find me at fault, saying trouble rode with such strangers. But I asked what else I might have done—slain them out of hand perhaps? And that shamed them, for though their hard life had brought a certain callousness to them, yet they still remembered the old days when a man's door stood open to the world, with bread and drink set always at the table as welcome to all travelers.

Pell was gravely injured and Aufrica, for all her skill, could not hold back the shadow of death, though she fought valiantly for his life. Jervon, though he had appeared strong and ready to fight, took a fever from his ill-tended wound, and lay with wandering wits and burning flesh for some days. Pell had slipped beyond help and was laid in our small Field of Memory (where four others of our people slept) before he spoke again rationally.

I had been standing by his bed, watching and wondering if he, too, in the fierce burning of the fever would go from us, and thinking that would be a sad waste of a man, when he opened his eyes and looked straight at me. Then he frowned a little as he spoke:

"I remember you—"

His greeting was odd, but many times a person out of grave illness carries half dreams which are confused.

I brought a cup of herb drink and put my arm about his shoulders to raise him to drink of it.

"You should," I told him as he sipped. "I brought you here."

He said nothing more, though he still watched me with that faint frown. Then he asked:

"My lord Pell?"

I used the saying of the country people. "He has gone ahead."

His eyes closed, but I saw his mouth tighten. What Pell had been to him, I did not know. But they were at least battle comrades, and I guessed that he had done much to try to save him.

But I did not know what to say then. For to some sorrow is a silent thing which they must battle alone, and I thought perhaps Jervon was such a one.

However, I surveyed him as he lay there. Though he was wasted and gaunt from fever, and perhaps from earlier hardship, he was a man of good presence, tall, if spare of body, but, like my father a swordsman born. He was a Dalesman in that his hair was golden-brown (lighter than the skin of his face and hands which were darkly browned by the weather) and his features well cut. I thought I could like what I saw, save there was no reason to believe that I would ever have any closer contact to continue or deepen such liking. He would heal and then ride away, as had my father and Elyn.

# 3

# Tarnished Silver

YET JERVON did not heal as speedily as we had thought, for the fever weakened him, mainly in his wounded arm. Although he worked grimly at exercises to restore full use, still he could not order fingers to tighten to grip as they should. Patiently, or outwardly so, he would toss a small stone from hand to hand, striving to grip it with full strength.

However he took part in our work in the dale, both in the ragged fields and as sentry in the hills. And in this much we were favored, none trailed him.

We gathered at night to listen to his accounts of the war, though he spoke of dales, and towns, fords, and roads of which we had never heard, since those of Wark had never traveled far overland until they had been uprooted. By his account the struggle was going ill for the Dales. All the southern coast holdings had long since been overrun, and only a ragged, desperate force had withdrawn to the north and the west. It had been during that last withdrawal that his own people had been overwhelmed.

"But the Lords have made a pact," he told us, "with those who have powers greater—or so they say—than those of sword and bow. In the spring of this Year of the Gryphon they met with the Were-Riders of the wastes and those will fight hereafter with us."

I heard a low whistle or two, for what he spoke of was indeed an unheard-of thing—that Dalesmen should treat with the Old Ones. For of those the Were-Riders were. Though the Dales had lain mainly empty at the coming of the settlers, yet there were still a few of those who had held this land eons before. And not all of them were such unseen presences as my mother had dealt with, but rather resembled men.

Such were the Were-Riders, men, in part, in other ways different. There were many tales about them and none which could be sworn to, since they were always reported third- or fourth-hand. But that they were a formidable force to enlist on our side no one could deny. And such was our hatred for the invaders—those Hounds of Alizon—that we would have welcomed monsters if they would march with our host.

The long summer became fall and still Jervon worked to restore skill to his hand. Now he took to combing the hills with his crossbow, bringing back game, yet not going as a hunter. He was a lone man, courteous and pleasant. Still as my father had been, one who erected a barrier between himself and the world.

He stayed with Aufrica until his hurt was healed as well as she could manage, then went to make a hut for himself a little apart. Never was he one with us. Nor did I see much of him, save at a distance. But since my skill with the bow was in much demand to lay up meat to be dried and salted (we had found a salt lick, a very precious thing), I was not often in our straggle of huts.

Then one day I slid down a steep bank to break my thirst at a bubbling spring. There he lay. He must have been staring up at the sky, but at my coming he started up, his hand to sword hilt. But what he said to me was no greeting:

"I remember where I saw you first—but that cannot be so!" He shook his head as if completely puzzled. "How can you ride with Franklyn of Edale and also be here? Yet I would have sworn—"

I turned to him eagerly. For if he had seen Elyn, then indeed he would be bewildered by our likeness.

"That was my brother, born at one birth with me! Tell me, when did you see him—and where?"

The puzzlement faded from Jervon's face. He sat working his hand upon a stone as he always did. "It was at the last muster at Inisheer. Franklyn's men have devised a new way of war. They hide out in the land and allow the enemy to push past them, then harry them from the rear. It is a very dangerous way." Jervon paused, looked at me quickly, as if he wished he had not been so frank.

I answered his thought. "Being his father's son Elyn would glory in such danger. I never believed he could be found far from action."

"They have won great renown. And your brother is far from the least among them. For all his youth they name him Horn Leader. He did not speak at our council, but he stood at Franklyn's shoulder—and they say by Franklyn's will he is handfasted to the Lady Brunissende, who is Franklyn's heiress."

I could think of Elyn as a fighter and one of re-

31

nown, but the news that he was hand-fasted made me blink. Seasons had passed, yet I saw him still in my mind the boy who had ridden out of Wark, untaught in the ways of war, yet eager to see sword bared against sword.

Moved by the thought of time, I wondered about myself. If Elyn was a man, then I was a woman. Yet of the ways of a woman I had little knowledge. In my father's day I had learned to be a son, from Aufrica to be a Wise Woman. But I had never been myself—me. Now I was a hunter, a fighter if the need demanded. But I was not a woman.

"Yes, you are very like," Jervon's voice broke through my straying thoughts. "This is a strange, hard life for a maid, Lady Elys."

"In these days all is awry," I made swift answer. For I was not minded to let him think *I* felt that there was aught strange in what I did, or was. It questioned my pride and that I would not allow.

"And it seems this must be so forever!" Now he looked at his hand, flexing his fingers.

My eyes followed his. "You do better!" It was true, he had more control.

"Slow, but it mends," he agreed. "When I can use arms again I must ride."

"Whither?"

At that he smiled with a touch of grimness. But, limited though it was, that change of expression made him for an instant like another person. And I suddenly wondered what Jervon would be if the darkness of war were lifted from him and he free to seek what he wanted of life.

"Whither *is* right, Lady Elys. For I know not where this dale of yours lies in relation to those I rode with. And when I set forth it will be a case of hunting to find—rather than be found—by the enemy."

"The snows are early in this high country." I drank from a palmful of water. It was very cold, already there might have been ice touched at its source. "We are shut in when the passes close."

He looked to the peaks, from one to another.

"That I can believe. You have wintered here though."

"Yes. It means tight-pulled belts toward spring, but each year we make better of what we have, lay in more supplies. There were two extra fields planted this year. The mills have ground twice as much barley this past month. Also we have salted down six wild cows, the which we were not lucky enough to have last year."

"But what do you do when snow closes in?"

"We keep within. At first we suffered from lack of wood." I could shudder even now at the memory of that and the three deaths which came of it. "Then Edgir found the black stone which burns. He did it by chance, having set his night-hunter-fire against such a stone—it caught afire and kept him well warmed. So now we haul in baskets of it—you must have seen the bins against each hut. We spin, we weave, we carve deer's horn and wood, and make the small things which keep life from being too harsh and gray.

"There is a songsmith—Uttar. He tells not only the old tales, but fashions new ones from our own wanderings. He also has made a lap-harp to play upon. No, we are not lacking life and interest during the cold."

"And this is what you have known all your life, Lady Elys?" There was a note in his voice I did not understand.

"In Wark there was more. We had the sea and trade with Jurby. Also—Aufrica and I—we have much to keep us busy."

"Yet you are what you are—no fisher maid, nor farm wench."

"No—I am Wise Woman, hunter, warrior— And now I must be about my hunting."

I arose, disturbed at that note in his voice. Did he dare to *pity* me? I was Elys and I had much more within the hollow of my hand than perhaps any dale lady. Though I might not have my mother's learning, yet there were places I could go, things I might do, which would turn such fragile flowers into quivering, white-faced nothings!

So I left him with a small wave of the hand, and went seeking hill deer. Though I had little luck that

33

day and brought back only two forest fowl for all my tramping.

Through all these days I never ceased to draw out the cup binding Elyn and me and look upon it each day. Though I did this secretly. It was on the fourth day after my chance meeting with Jervon that I drew aside the covering and was startled. For the gleaming beauty was dimmed, as if some faint tarnishing had spread a film across it.

Aufrica, seeing that, cried out. But I was silent, only inside me was a sharp thrust, not of pain, but of fear which was in itself a kind of pain. I rubbed hastily at the metal, to no purpose. This was not caused by any dust, or moisture condensing on the surface, but an inner clouding. It was not lifeless and dead, which would mean Elyn was beyond any help of mine, but that he was in danger this was the first warning.

I spoke to Aufrica. "I would far-see—"

She went to the rude cupboard now the safekeeping place of all her painfully gathered stores. From there she took a large shell with a well-polished interior.

Also she gathered small vials and a leathern bottle and a copper pot no bigger than my hand. Into the last she dropped powder pinch by pinch. Then began to combine in a beaker a drop of this, a spoon measure of that, until she had a dark red liquid washing there as she turned it around and around to mix it.

"It is ready."

I pulled a splinter from the firebox, dipped it to the flame, and with it ignited the contents of the pot. Greenish smoke, strong scented, curled up. Aufrica poured the crimson stream into the dragon cup, taking care it reached almost to the inner rim yet did not overflow. Then quickly she repoured it into the shell basin.

Before that I sat. The scented smoke made me feel a little lightheaded, as if, did I not use my will to remain on the stool, I might float away. Now I leaned forward and looked into the ruby pool in the shell.

This was not the first time I had used the power of

scrying, yet never before had it been of such importance to me. So I was tense and willed the sight to come quickly and clearly. The red of the liquid faded and I saw, as one looking into a room from a far distance. For it was a room which was pictured there. The details, though small, were clear and sharp.

By the shadows it was night, yet a candle-holder as tall as a man's shoulder stood at one end of a curtained bed. In that a fist-thick candle burned bright. The bed was rich, its curtains patterned by a skillful needle, and those curtains had not been closed. Resting therein against pillows was a young girl of the Dales people. Her face was fine of feature and very fair, her unbound hair ribbons of gold about her shoulders. She slept—or at least her eyes were closed.

In all it was a scene of rich splendor such as might be from some tale a songsmith created.

But the girl was not alone for, even as I watched, one moved out of the shadows. As the candlelight fell full upon his face, I saw it was my brother, though older than I remembered him. He glanced at the sleeping girl as if he feared her waking.

Then he went to the wall where was a window. That was closed by a great shutter with three bars locked across it, as if he, or those who had closed it, wanted to make very sure it could not be opened in haste.

Elyn brought forth a dagger and began to pry here and there. On his face was intent concentration, as if what he did now was of such importance that nothing else mattered.

He wore a loose bedchamber robe girdled about him, and, as he raised his arms to lever with the dagger, the wide sleeves fell back to show his bare, well-muscled arms. On the bed the covers were tumbled, the pillow dented where he must recently have lain. Yet he worked with such dire determination that I could feel it as I watched.

Beyond that barrier was something calling him. And —I also felt the faint, far touch of that call. It was like the fiery end of a burning splinter touched to my bare flesh! From it my mind flinched as if I felt the actual pain of a burn. Flinched, and so broke the power of the scry bowl, so the picture vanished.

I was breathing hard and fast as if I had fled some danger. As indeed I had. For what pulled Elyn into such action was peril indeed. And it was not of his world at all—unless he had greatly altered since we drank farewell from the dragon cup.

"Danger—" Aufrica did not ask a question, she stated a fact.

"Elyn—he is drawn by something of a—a *dark* Great One!"

"As yet it is only a warning." She pointed to the cup. "A faint shadow—"

"But the warning is for me. If he is fair caught in some ensorcelment he will not be easily kept from the trap. He is not my mother's son, but my father's. There is none of the gift in him."

"True said. And now you will go to him."

"I will go, hoping that I may be in time."

"You have all that I could give you." Her voice was touched with pain. "You have what came to you by right of birth. But you have not what armed my lady. Daughter of the heart have you been to me, me who had no child of my flesh, since I was not one to tread the path your mother walked in her time. I cannot stay you from going, but with you you take my sun—"

She bowed her head and hid her face in her hands. For the first time I noted, with surprise, that those were thin and wrinkled, showing more clearly the approach of age than did her face. For she was one of those with good bones, whose skin was clear and tight. Yet in that moment she huddled on her stool as one beaten, all the passing years pressing upon her at once as a burden under which she was like to sink.

"Mother-kin have you been to me." I rested my hands on her hunched shoulders. "No more have I ever asked than to be daughter-kin to you, Wise Woman. But in this thing I have no choice."

"That I know also. For it is in my mind that your Lady Mother thought that this would be your path in life, to serve others, even as she did in her time. I shall fear for you—"

"Not so!" I interrupted her. "For to think fear is to give it life. You must rather work with power, saying that I go not to defeat, but victory."

Aufrica raised her head, and seemed to banish by will her trouble. I knew that she now determined her strength would be as a force of swordsmen to guard me. And the strength of Aufrica as I well knew (I who had seen her battle death in her time and win) was a thing to be reckoned high.

"Where will you seek?" She spoke briskly as one who would plan.

"For that—the casting."

Again she went to her store place and this time brought out a much-folded cloth to be smoothed flat. It was divided with lines of gold into four quarters, and those quarters in turn to small triangles by lines of red all running through the center inscribed with runes no man could longer read but which were Words of Power.

Then she produced a chain of gold from which hung pendant a small ball of crystal. On the other end of the chain was a band ring she slipped on her finger. She then stood by the table, stretching forth her hand until the ball was directly over that centerpoint on the cloth. Though her hand held steady, the ball began to swing back and forth. Then it altered that swing, traveling only along one of the red lines, back and forth. I studied and remembered.

So—south and west I must go. And soon, or, as I had warned Jervon, the snow would come to close the passes and there would be no traveling at all.

Now the ball hung motionless. Aufrica drew it up by its chain into her hand and put it away in a small bag as I refolded the cloth.

"Tomorrow," I said.

"It is best," she agreed. Straightaway she went once more to her storage place and began taking stock there. I knew she would send me forth as well armed with those things of the Wise Learning as she could.

But I went to seek Omund in his hut. Since all were aware that Aufrica and I had ways of seeing the unseeable and dealing with matters not open to most, my news would not sound unbelievable to him. Though we did not explain to any the methods we used to gain our foreknowledge. I merely told him that through the learning of a Wise Woman I had discovered my brother was in trouble. And that trouble came not from war but was of the Old Ones. Therefore, since this was a birth geas long laid on me, I must go to his aid.

Omund nodded his head when I was done, though his womenfolk, as always, gave me side looks of ill-confidence.

"It is as you say, Lady, there is no choice for you. You leave us soon then?"

"With tomorrow's dawn. The snow may come early this year."

"True. Well, Lady, you have dealt fair and fine with us, as did your Lady Mother and the Lord, your father, when they dwelt among us. But we are neither blood nor kin of yours. And both those are ties we must answer when the call comes. For all your aid in the past we are thankful and—" He arose stiffly to his feet and went to a box-chest he had made. "This is small enough return for all you have done, but it will keep you warm of nights in this harsh land."

He brought out a journey cloak which must have been the work of many days. It was fashioned of the shaggy hair of the high mountain goats left on the hides, yet dyed a soft, dark purple like the haze of twilight—a color which might be accident of some chance combination of dyes and not to be found again. It had a beauty which was rare in our present lives. Nor would I believe that any lady would have a winter covering to better it.

My thanks I could only make in words, yet I was sure he understood what this meant to me. For in my life I had many useful things and things well made, but seldom did those combine with beauty also. But he only smiled and clasped my hand in both of his, bending his grayed head to touch his lips to my calloused fingers as if, indeed, I was his lady.

In that moment I realized that, strange though I had felt myself in Wark always, yet, in a way these were my people and I was losing something now. Still not all felt as Omund, and those even of his household were glad to see me go.

With the cloak over my arm I went back to Aufrica —there being none other here to take private leave of. There, somewhat to my surprise, I found Jervon. He was seated by the table which was now bare of all Aufrica's things of power, though she was still fitting packets into a shoulder bag. And he seemed more at ease than I had seen him before, in his hand a cup of Aufrica's blended herb brewing sweetened with wild honey.

He arose as I entered and there was an eagerness about him I had not seen before.

"The Wise Woman says you ride forth, my lady."

"I have that which must be done."

"Which I have also, having lingered long enough. Therefore, these being days when no man rides alone if he can help it, there being a need for eyes to watch both sides of the road, we shall fare together."

Nor did he ask that, rather he spoke as if it were already decided. That irked me. Yet I knew that he spoke the truth—that to travel in company, and with one who knew far better than I the dangers wherein I would travel, would be an aid I dared not, simply out of pride, refuse. So I schooled my voice, but I asked:

"And if I ride not in your direction, swordsman?"

He shrugged. "Have I not said I know not where my lord may now be? If you seek your brother to the south and west, there shall I also find news of my banner. Though I warn you, Lady, we may be heading directly into the open mouth of the dragon, or perhaps I should say—the open jaws of the Hounds!"

"Of which your knowledge shall warn us," I retorted. I was determined that this would be no farfaring in which I was to be treated as a fine lady from a Dale house, guarded and swaddled with care. If we rode together, it was as battle comrades, free and equal. But how I was to say this I did not yet know.

Aufrica, seeing the cloak, came forward with an exclamation of delight that I would have such a fine protection against the cold. And she straightaway brought out a box brooch to fasten it. Nor did I need telling that within the lid of that was set as powerful a travel spell as she could evoke.

Jervon put down his cup.

"With the dawn then, Lady? We do not go afoot— I have the horse which bore me hither, and the one which was Pell's."

"Dawn," I agreed. And I was pleased at the thought of horses, for they would mean swifter passage. South and west—but to where—and how far?

# 4

## *Coomb Frome*

PERFORCE we took the road which had brought Jervon as there was no other trace across the wilderness. And, since his coming, none had traveled it.

It was a very old road, and here and there were signs it had been worked upon—by man? I thought not, for those before us here had been only herdsmen and hunters, wandering folk. Which meant this was a way of the Old Ones.

"This comes within a league of the Ford," Jervon said. "But there it loops away from the sea. We turned into it only because it gave better footing for the race we were forced to. But where it comes from and to where it leads—" He shrugged.

"It is of the Old Ones, and who knows their reasons?" That was a Dales' answer, yet I knew there was always logic in the remains of the Old Ones—though it might not be ours.

"You are not of the Dales." He sent that statement at me as he might a well-aimed crossbow bolt, a deadly one.

Deadly? Why had that thought come to me? But I made truthful answer.

"I was born in Wark, therefore I am of the Dales. But my parents came from overseas. Yet they were not of Alizon, but of some nation already at war with the Hounds. So that when my father heard of the invasion he straightaway rode to war. Since we have heard naught since, and it has been many seasons now, he is likely dead. My mother died at the birthing of Elyn and me. That is my breeding, swordsman."

"No, you have nothing of the Dales in you," he continued, almost as if he had not heard my words. "They say things of you, these people once of Wark—"

"As they say of any Wise Woman," I countered. And I did not doubt that many things had been said of me, surely not all to my favor, for with Aufrica alone had I been close. And such as Omund's women had long looked askance as I passed. I was not wedded wife, not like to be—for that state goes not with my gifts. That, too, made a gulf. Had we had more able-bodied men I might have been pushed to a troublemaking decision. For I was not like to tend the hearth of any man of Wark.

"More than Wise Woman, they say. They speak behind their hands of dealings with the Old Ones." There was no tone of awe nor trace of aversion in his voice, only curiosity. He was like a warrior confronted by a new weapon who would ask questions concerning it.

"Would I might say that was so! One able to bargain with the Old Ones need not live as you saw us living. Do not men say that the power can bring all things—build Keep in a night, dash an enemy army into nothingness, make a rich garden grow on barren rock? Have you seen that behind us?"

To my surprise he laughed. "Far from it, shield-maid. But I do not decry the learning of a Wise Woman—whether she be of a village or one of the Houses

41

of Dames. Also, I think that the Old Ones might not be interested in our petty squabbles—or so must our strivings seem to them—and they could be inclined to treat summarily any who disturb their rest."

"You must seek them, they come not uncalled." And in that I might have been foreseeing without knowing it.

The country continued barren and we kept to an even pace which did not tax our mounts, for to be afoot here would be dire. At noon we turned from that old road way and ate journey bread, drank from a stream, and let our mounts graze for a space. Jervon lay on his back, looking up into the laced branches of a gnarled tree which hung, with just a thin tatter of leaves, over the bank above the spring.

"I am truly of the Dales," he said. "My father was a third son and so landless. After the custom he took oath to the Lord of Dorn, who was kinsman to his mother, and became his Marshal of Horse. My mother was a damozel of the Lady Guida's household. I was well trained. My father had it in his mind to strike out, when I was old enough, to the northern wild country, and seek his own land. He had four or five heads of households pledged to back him.

"Then came the invaders and there was no thought of riding north, only of trying to preserve what we already had. Dorn was in the path of the first inward thrust. They took the Keep in five days, for they had new weapons which spat fire and even ate rock. I had ridden to Haverdale to beg help. We caught up with two survivors on the road three days later. Dorn was gone, erased as if it had never been. We did not believe them at first. I took to the country that night and reached a place from which I could look down. What I saw might have been a place of the Old Ones, so time tumbled you could not tell wall from courtyard."

He spoke without emotion, perhaps time had dulled it so this seemed now to have happened to another man. This is a merciful healing when it happens. Now he paused and, though his eyes seemed to search the branches over him, yet I knew he saw something far different.

"I stayed with Haverdale and took oath. We could not hold the western road, not with the devil weapons of the Hounds on it. Though those did not last long. They could be destroyed by desperate men and fire, and they were. It would seem that the Hounds had no others, at least we did not see them crunching over the countryside again. But they had made good use of them. Every major Dale hold in the south was gone—every one!" The hand lying on his chest balled into a fist, though there was still no emotion in his voice.

"There was no one leader to whom all the Dale lords would rally. The Hounds had made sure of that —Remard of Dorn, Myric of Gastendale, Dauch, Yonan —all the men of promise were either wiped out with their holds and their followers, or assassinated. The Hounds were well prepared, they knew all our weak points. And it would seem we had more of those than defenses. The lords did not unite and they had no trouble plucking them off one by one as they would pluck ripe fruit from a heavily laden branch.

"We could only run, and perhaps hit, and then run again. And we would have all been bleaching bones had not the Four Lords come out of the north and beat some order and sense into us. They made all see we must unite or die. So there was the confederation and they made the pact with the Were-Riders.

"It has been long, but the tide is turning now. We have driven them back dale by dale—though they rally at times—we who were at Ingra Ford can say that. But in time I think the Hounds will howl instead of bay and we shall have a final accounting. Though what will be left then— For there are many lords dead and dales war swept. High Hallack will be another land altogether. Perhaps there will be an overrule of the Four —no, Three—for Skirkar is dead and he leaves no son to raise hold banner. Yes, it will be a different land."

"What will you do? Remain Marshal at Haverdale?"

"If I live that long, you mean?" He smiled. "We do

not plan futures for ourselves any more. There will be some to survive, but as a fighting man I cannot say I shall be among them. I do not know what will chance if I live to see full victory. For all the days since I have been counted a man I have been at war. I can hardly remember what peace means. So—no, I do not think I shall give peace-oath to Haverdale. Perhaps I may even follow my father's dream, go north and seek land of my own. But I plan not. To live through another day takes all the wits a man has."

"There are tales of the north and east, that there are more remainders of the Old Ones there." I was trying to remember what little I had heard of that country.

"True enough. So perhaps it is just as well not to go troubling in those quarters. It is time we ride, shield-maid."

Nightfall found us in a place of rocks and there we huddled without any betraying fire. I offered the over-protection of Omund's cloak as I would to any comrade. And he accepted cloth-company as he might had I been Elyn and not Elys. So that the warmth of our bodies under the cloak let us sleep snug in spite of frost without.

Another day's ride and we were at the Ford. The wrack of the fight was still strewn there. Though there was a funeral pyre at one side. Jervon raised bared sword in salute.

"Haverdale did that. They paid death honors. Therefore they gained forces and returned." He dismounted and went searching among discarded weapons, returning with a dozen crossbow bolts to replenish his small stock. He also had a fine dagger with a gemmed hilt and a blade which, for all its outlaying in the weather, had not been dimmed by any rust.

"Hound work, of their best," he said, putting it into his own belt.

"Now," he swung into the saddle once again, "there is a traders' road here, it swings south to Trevamper. Though that town may not now stand."

Though it was close to dusk we did not camp at the Ford. That was too close to the pyre, too full of memories for my companion. We rode on until he turned off into a thicket. That was a screen for a place where rings of stones were set about the ash of old fires, and some hacked poles made rude shelters.

"Our camp." He stirred the ashes with boot toe. "Long dead. I think it will be safe to stay."

Once more we dared not light a fire. But this night the moon was bright and clear. I knew that I must look upon my talisman for this search. Though I could not be private, and to let my secret into the keeping of another was hard. Yet it was necessary to know how it fared with Elyn.

Thus when we had eaten, I got out the cup and took away its shielding cloth. Almost I dropped it. For that tarnishing cloud, which had been only a mist, had now deepened about the stem and lower part of the bowl into a black stain. So I knew that ill had come upon Elyn. But, though he was in grave danger he still lived, and would until the cup was entirely black.

"What is it?"

I wished I did not need to answer, but there was no way of escaping Jervon's interest.

"This warns of my brother's danger. Before it was only a clouding, now—see this black? As it rises up the cup, so his danger grows. If the cup be all black, he is dead."

"A third of the way," he returned. "Have you any way of learning what this danger may be?"

"None—save it is not the chance of war—but bound up in the ways of power. He is caught in some ensorcelment."

"The Dalesmen do not take to sorcery save as the Wise Women practice it. And the Hounds have their own kind, not rooted in our beliefs at all. So—the Old Ones—"

But I could not think of any way Elyn could so have aroused some ancient evil. He had never had any interest in such matters. I tried to recall my far-seeing— of that bedchamber where the girl had slept while my brother wrenched and levered at bars across a shuttered window.

45

"Can you far-see?" Jervon asked.

"Not here. I have not the proper things—" Then I wondered.

I had been so schooled by Aufrica that instinctively I thought of all such seeking in patterns she set. But she had always insisted that I had inheritances of stronger powers.

The tie between Elyn and me was close; we were born at one birth; when we looked upon each other we might be looking into a mirror. Therefore—

"Give me the water bottle!"

Jervon passed it over. I took out one of the strips of soft-beaten inner bark which I carried in my pouch for wounds. Into this I rubbed pinches of three of the herbs Aufrica had supplied and then wet it with water from the bottle, washing my hands carefully with the mixture.

Having so purified myself, I took up the cup. Though it held no liquid, I looked into it as I had into the shell basin, striving to shut out of my mind all save Elyn, thus search out where he was and what he did.

Suddenly it was as if I were *in* the cup, for about me was a silver-white light. Only for a moment did that bedazzle me. Then I was able to see more clearly. Around me stood tall pillars like the trunks of forest trees, save that these were smooth and polished, their slimness unbroken by any branch. Nor did they support any roof; overhead was nothing but moon and star-hung sky.

These pillars stood not in rows, but rather in a spiral so that one entering among them would walk around and around, in and in, to whatever lay at their heart. At that moment I knew a vast fear, like none I had known before, so I could not even think. For what waited at the heart of that spiral was something so far from the way of life I knew that it was utter terror.

Then—that changed. It was as if it suddenly put on a mask or shield. The terror was cut off, and in its place—a drawing—a sensation of wonder, of the need to see the source of that wonder. Yet because I had earlier felt that overwhelming aura of what really lurked there I was repelled and not ensorceled.

Out into the open came a figure, mailed, helmed, with sword at hip, riding a war steed. He dismounted, dropping the reins as if he cared not now whether it should wander or not. And he moved toward the opening of the spiral as if he were called.

I tried to cry out, to force myself between Elyn and that gateway to a darkness far worse than death. But I could not move. My brother approached the beginning of the spiral—

"Elys!" Hands on my shoulders, shaking me. I sat hunched over the cup—the empty cup— The moon was light but there were no pillars, no spiral.

I raised the cup hurriedly to eye level, more than half fearing that that black shadow would have crept higher. For if Elyn was in that pillared way—how could he be saved? But the stain was no greater than it had been before.

"What did you see?" Jervon demanded. "You—it was as if you looked upon some great horror and you cried upon your brother's name as if you would pull him out of death's hold by voice alone."

Jervon knew more of this land than I; surely he would know of the spiraled way—the quickest path! For such a thing of menace would be noted to Dalesmen.

"Listen." As I covered the cup to stow it away, I told him of that earlier vision—my brother laboring to open the window, then of this later one. "Where lies such a place?"

"Not in Trevamper, or near it," he returned promptly. "But the barred window—somewhere—sometime I have heard of that." He rubbed his forehead as if so to summon back a wisp of memory.

"Window—barred window! Yes—the Keep of Coomb Frome! There is an old legend, that from one window in the center tower men can see the far hills. And if they do this at some one hour—they take horse and ride—and from that riding they do not return. Nor can those who seek them thereafter ever find them again.

So Coomb Frome was no longer a lord's house but kept only as a garrison and the window in the tower was close shut. But that all happened in my grandfather's time."

"It could be that Coomb Frome is once more a lord's hold. Did you not say my brother was hand-fasted? By what I have seen he is now wed. Yet he left his lady and went forth to search for that—! I ride to Coomb Frome!"

So we came to that Keep, but our reception there was a surprise. Though when I was first hailed by out-post men as Lord Elyn I did not deny it. It was in my mind to learn what I could of my brother before I asked questions. So I said I had been on scout and they would hear my report in due time. Perhaps a lame explanation, yet they did not protest it, only seemed glad to have me back.

Nor did Jervon deny my story. He looked to me with a question in his eyes, and then away, as if he were willing to accept the role I assumed. I pretended a great desire to see my lady wife, for I had been right, Elyn was wedded to the Lady Brunissende.

Men smiled at that, and some laughed a little and whispered one to the other. I could guess they passed such jests as men do when the newlywed are in their company. Only the eldest, a man of some rank, said my lady had taken hard my going forth and had since kept her chamber. At this I played the role of great concern and set heel to horse rib in urging for speed.

Thus I came into that same chamber I had seen in my vision. And the girl of my dream lay still on the bed, though there was with her now an older woman who had something of the look of Aufrica. So I judged she might be of the Wise company. The girl cried out:

"Elyn!" And started up, running to me, her night-robe all awry, her eyes puffed with past tears, her cheeks tracked by new ones. But the woman stared straight at me; then she raised her hand and made a sign I knew well, so that before I thought, I answered it.

Her eyes went very wide. But Brunissende was upon
me, her hands reaching for my shoulders, calling upon
my brother's name, demanding to know where I had
been and why I had left her. I put up my hands to
hold her a little off for this welcome I found difficult
to answer.

Then she pulled away, looking into my face wildly,
terror growing in her eyes.

"You are—you are changed! My dear lord—what have
they done to you?" She began to laugh shrilly and
struck out at me, her nails marking my face before I
could catch her hand, screaming I was not as I had
been.

The woman reached her quickly and, bringing her a
little around, slapped her face. So the screaming broke
abruptly and Brunissende looked from one to the other
of us, rubbing her cheek, yet when she faced me she
shivered.

"You are not Elyn." This time the woman spoke.
Then she recited words which I also knew. But before she completed that spell, I interrupted.

"I am Elys. Did he never speak of me?"

"Elys—Elys—" Brunissende repeated the name. "But
Elys is his sister! And you are a man with the seeming of my lord—who has come to deceive me evilly."

"I am Elys. If my brother said aught of me, you
also know that I shared his upbringing in part. Sword
and shield-work I learned even as he did in his childhood. Though when we were grown we went sepa-
rate ways. However, there was a bond between us, and
when I was warned that he was in peril, I came, even
as he would have come had he heard I walked into
danger."

"But—but how did you know he was gone—lost in
the hills? No messenger has ridden from here. We have
kept it secret lest worse happen if it were known."
Brunissende watched me now with the same side-look
I had seen in other women. And I thought that, mar-
riage-sister though she be, the time might well come
when she would like my room rather than my company. But if she were Elyn's choice then she had my

49

favor, save that now my first duty lay not with her but with my missing brother.

But her woman drew a step closer to me, all the time studying my face as if I bore there in bright paint some sign of who or what I truly was.

"It is the truth, my lady," she said slowly. "The Lord Elyn has said little save that his father and mother were dead, and he had a sister who dwelt among the people who sheltered them from childhood. However—I believe now that he might have said far more and yet not told all." Again she made a certain sign and I answered it with deliberation, but added somewhat that she might know I was of no low level in her learning. Then she nodded as one come to the solving of a problem.

"The far-seeing it must have been then, my lady. So you must also know where he now ventures—"

"It is sorcery of the Old Ones." I addressed her rather than Brunissende. "And of the Black not the White. It began with this—"

I pushed past the Lady Brunissende who still looked at me with a lack of full understanding to that window at which I had seen my brother labor with bars and bolts long rusted into place. It was close shut now as if he had never worked upon it. But when I laid hand to the lower bar I heard a choked cry and turned my head.

The Lady Brunissende cowered against the bed, both hands to her mouth, with nothing but witless terror in her eyes. She gave another muffled cry and swooned back into the tumbled covers.

# 5

## *The Curse of Ingaret*

THE WISE WOMAN went to her quickly, then looked to me again.

"It is but a swoon, and she is better not hearing what you would say, for she is frightened of such things—the learning."

"Yet you serve her."

"Ah, but I am her foster mother and she does not reckon what I do. But from her childhood she has feared the Curse, for it has lain heavy on her House."

"The Curse?"

"What lies beyond that—waiting—" She pointed to the window.

"Tell me, for I am not one who swoons. But, first, Wise Woman, what is your name?"

She smiled and I smiled in return at what we both knew, that she had one name for the world and one for the inner life.

"No, you are not one unable to bear the worst which may be told or shown you. As for my name—here I am Dame Wirtha—I am also Ulrica—"

"Dame?" For the first time I noted she did not wear the rich-colored robes of a Lord's household, but rather gray, and that the wimple of one of the abbeys covered all but her face. Yet I had heard that the Dames and the Old Knowledge did not meet. Also that those of the abbeys did not go beyond their enclosures after their final vows were taken.

"Dame," she repeated. "War upsets all. The House of Kantha Twice Born was overrun by the Hounds this year past. And since I escaped I came to Brunissende —as I took vows only after she was handfasted. Also Kantha Twice Born had the Old Learning herself in her time and her daughters are of a different thought

51

than those of other abbeys. But we have shared names
—or do you have another?"

I shook my head. There was something of Aufrica
in this Dame, but more which was herself alone. And
I knew I could trust her.

"I was Blessed at my first naming, given after the
custom of my mother's people—"

"The Witches of Estcarp! Would you had now what
they can control, for your need will be great if you
think to do what brought you here."

"Tell me of this Curse, for it must be that which
has taken Elyn."

"There is a record that the First of the House of
Ingaret, from whom my lady is descended, had a taste
for strange knowledge, yet not the patience nor the
discipline to follow the known roads. Therefore he
took risks such as no prudent men would think on.

"By his lone he went into the places of the Old
Ones and from such a journey he brought back a wife.
It was in this very chamber that they lay together,
but they had no children and the lord began to fret
for he would have a son to follow him. He took steps
to prove that the fault was not his—siring a son and
then a daughter on women he kept in secret. Could
any man be greater fool than to think he could hide
such matters?

"He came hither one night to take his pleasure with
his lady wife and found her sitting in a great chair,
like that in which he sat when he gave justice in the
hall. Before her on stools sat the women he had used
to beget the babes, and they were as if dazed, staring
straight before them, while on their knees rested their
children.

"When he faced his lady, blustering, demanding to
know what she did and why, she smiled at him very
sweetly, and said that she but saw to his comfort that
he might not have to journey forth in night and ill
weather to seek those to satisfy his body—she had
brought them under his roof.

"Then she arose and he found he could not move.
She put off the fine robes he had given her, and the

52

jewels he had set upon her, all these she tossed to the floor. Straightaway they became torn and tattered rags, broken base metal and glass. Then, with her body bare and beautiful in the moonlight, she walked to this very window and drew herself up on the sill.

"Thereupon she turned to look once more on Ingaret and she said words which down the years have never been forgot:

" 'You shall desire, you shall seek, and in the seeking you shall be lost. What you had you threw away, and it shall call through the years to others, and they shall also seek, but that seeking shall avail no one.'

"Then she turned and leaped through the window. But when the Lord Ingaret, released from the spell which had held him, raced to look down—below there was nothing. It was as if her leap had carried her into another world.

"He gathered together then his chief men and he acknowledged on a raised war-shield the boy as his son, gave a daughter's necklet to the girl. Of their mothers—after that night they were ever maze-minded and did not live long. But the lord did not wed again. In the tenth year following he rose at night and rode out of Coomb Frome, nor was he seen again.

"Through the years other men, some lords, some heirs, some husbands of heiresses, all close to the rule of Coomb Frome, looked from this window at full moon, and then rode out—to be seen no more. Until the window was tight-barred and the family would come no more to this Keep. So that in the latter days none vanished so—until your brother."

"If it had been many years—then perhaps this which waits is the greater hungered. You have the needful for far-seeing?"

"You would try that here? The Dark Powers must have potent rooting within this very room."

Her warning was apt. I knew what I attempted would be highly dangerous. Yet it was needful.

"Within the moon-star—" I suggested.

She nodded, then hurried into an inner chamber. I turned to the saddlebags I had carried with me and brought out the cup. Almost I feared to drop its wrappings lest I see it black. But, although the dark tide had grown higher on the bright silver, yet there was the space of two fingers' breadth untouched at the top. Seeing that I had hope.

The Dame came forth with a wide basket in which were small jars and bottles. First she took up a finger of white chalk and, stooping, she drew, in sharp, sure lines, the five-point star on the floor in line with that barred window. At each point she set a white candle.

That done she looked upon the cup I held. And she drew a startled breath.

"Dragon scale—where got you such a thing of power, Lady?"

"It was fashioned by and for my mother before my birth. From it I was named, as was Elyn, from it we drank farewell, so that it now bears the stain of his danger."

"Power indeed had your mother, Lady, to bring such as that into being. I have heard that it could be done, but the price is high—"

"One she paid without question." And I knew pride as I answered.

"Yes, for only one of courage could do so. You are ready? I have given you such protection as I know."

"I am ready."

I waited until she poured within the cup a blend of liquids from two of her bottles. Then I stepped within the star while she lit the candles. As they burned brightly, I heard her croon the Summons. But her voice was very faint and far away, as if she were not almost within arm's-length but across a dale ridge.

But my eyes were on the interior of the cup where the liquid began to bubble. A mist from it filled my nostrils, though I did not turn my head aside. The mist drifted away and the liquid was a still mirror.

It was as if I were suspended in air, perhaps on wings. Below me was the spiral of the pillars. The curve of it wound around and around to a center heart. And in that heart were people. They stood so still —unbreathing. Not people then, but images, so finely wrought they seemed alive. They, too, were in a spiral, one very near the heart, the others curling outward. And the last in that line—

Elyn!

As I recognized him, something knew me, or at least that I spied upon it. Not anger, no, rather contempt, amusement, scorn that so small and weak a thing as I would trouble it. Yet it was also—

I exerted my will, was back again among the steadily burning candles.

"You saw him?"

"Yes. Also I know where to find him. And that must be done swiftly."

"Steel—weapons—will not save him."

"Be sure I know that. Yet before she has never taken one tied to such as me. She has grown sure of herself, very sure, and that may work against her."

Two things only, and small, but in my favor. Certainly no missing lord of Coomb Frome had before been sought by a Wise Woman blood-tied to him. Yet the time was so short. If Elyn stayed too long in that web he would be as those others, an image, not a man.

"There is a way privately from this Keep?" I asked.

"Yes. You would go at once?"

"I have no choice."

She gave me things from her own store, two amulets, herbs. Then she took me by a hidden way between the walls, made for escape should the tower be besieged.

And she had her own serving maid bring a horse. Thus I rode out at dawning, armed and mounted, pulled by the thin thread my far-seeing had spun. How far I must go I had no idea, so that I kept the horse to the best pace I could since time was now my enemy. I slipped past patrols, mainly by using the craft of a Wise Woman to distort their sight of me. At last I was in the wild country beyond which was a maze of sharp-cut ravines and thick brush, so that I had to dismount many times and find a way by breaking or sword-slashing a path.

After one such bout of labor I stood, my hand on

the saddle horn, resting before I pulled up again on the blowing horse. Then I knew I was being followed.

That such brush might conceal outlaws I was aware. Or even those from the Keep, mystified by their lord's seeming return and new disappearance, come to track me. Any interference might be fatal to Elyn.

At least in such broken country I could find cover from which to watch my back trail and decide what to do. Sword in hand, I urged my horse within a screen of brush so thick that even autumn loss of leaves did not make it transparent. There I waited.

Whoever came was a master at woodcraft. And I thought of how my brother had ridden with those who struck hard behind enemy lines. But he who advanced so silent-footed, whom I might not have seen had he not inadvertently startled a bird, was Jervon.

Jervon, whom I had in the main forgotten since I had arrived at the Keep. But why? He should be making his own plans to join his lord.

I stepped from behind my screen.

"What do you on this road, swordsman?"

"Road?" His face was shadowed by his helm but I saw his eyebrows tilt upward. So did he look when he was amused. Though amusement had not come often during the days we had been together. "I would not call this wilderness a road, but perchance my eyes have been deceived. As for what I do here, well, did I not earlier say that one does not ride alone when company is offered—not in these days?"

"You cannot go with me!" My voice was a little high as I answered. For I sensed the stubbornness in him. And the road I followed was to such a battle as perhaps he could not imagine, and in which he would be enemy instead of friend.

"Very well. Ride on, my lady—" He agreed so readily that my anger sparked.

"And have you trail behind? I tell you, Jervon, this is no place for you. What I do is the art of the Wise Women. And I must also face a curse of the Old Ones—one strong enough still to man-slay." I owed him the truth, for in no other way might I convince him that I was right.

But his expression did not change. "Have I not known this, or much of it, from the beginning? Go to war with your spells, but this is still debatable ground and there are human wolves as well as those strange menaces you have better knowledge of. What if you are attacked with steel and bolt before you reach your goal, or while you must keep your mind and strength for your sorcery?"

"You owe me no oath service. In fact you already have a lord. Seek him out as if your duty."

"No oath did I give you, Lady Elys. But I took oath to myself. I stand at your back while you ride this way. And do not look to cast some spell on me to bring my will to naught. The Dame at the Keep gave me this."

He reached within the throat of his mail shirt and drew forth a pendant of moon-silver wrought into a looped cross, and I knew he was right. Unless I expended on him strength I would need later, I could not overcome the protection that carried. But it was a shield for him where we went. Though I wondered at the Dame sending after me anyone unlearned in any Wise Craft.

"So be it," I surrendered. "But this I lay upon you —if you feel aught—any compulsion—say so at once. There are spells to turn friends into enemies and open gates to great peril."

"That I agree to."

Thus I did not ride alone for the rest of the day. And at nightfall, which came early at that season, we halted on a ridge top where there were two great spires of rock standing. Between them we dismounted.

"You know where you go?" Jervon had traveled in silence most of the afternoon. Were it not for the sound of his passage behind me from time to time, I might well have forgotten I had a trail companion.

"I am drawn." Though I did not explain farther. Now I was too much aware of something in this country before us, a troubling, an uneasiness, as if something which usually slumbered deep now stirred. And I was well aware, that learned as I was, I certainly could not provide an equal match for such as the Old Ones.

"Are we yet near or far?" he asked.

"Near—we must be near." For so I read that troubling. "Which means—you must remain here."

"Remember what I said." His hand was on the loop cross. "I follow where you lead."

"But in this country you need not fear any human," I began, then read in his eyes that no word of mine would move him. Short of attacking him with sword, or spell, I had no chance at staying him. Though I wondered at his stubbornness, for which I could see no reason.

"You face a peril you cannot understand." I put into that warning all the force I could muster. "We deal now not with those who fight with steel and strength of arm, but with other weapons you cannot dream of—"

"Lady, since I saw what the weapons of the Hounds did to Dorn, I keep an open mind concerning all and any arms." Again there seemed to be a quirk of humor in his speech. "Also, since that day I have been, in a sense, living on time not mine, since by rights I should have died with those I loved and who made up my world. Thus I do not wager my life—for that I feel I no longer own. And there is in me a great desire to see how you wage war with these unheard-of strengths and unknown arms you speak of so knowingly. If we are close—let us to the battlefield then!"

There was so much decision in his words that I could not find any to answer him. But went to look downslope before us, seeking the safest path, for we were about to descend into a country which stretched wide and unusually dark, even though twilight still lay along the ridges.

What I saw was surely one of the Old Roads, or rather a trail, and that ran in the right direction so we could follow it. It was a narrow way, suffering us only at intervals to ride abreast. And it led into a woodland, wandering back and forth between trees with trunks so huge in girth that they must have been centuries growing.

Very still was this wood, only now and then the sigh of falling leaves. But never the cry of a night bird, nor rustle of ground animal such as was normal. And always the feeling of something awakening slowly.

"We are waited—" Jervon's voice was low, yet it was almost like a shout in my ears. "We are watched—"

So he was sensitive enough to feel it too. Still, as yet, there was no arising of menace, no threat in that stir. Just the sense that our coming registered in some way.

"As I warned you." For the last time I tried to move Jervon to withdraw before it was too late. "We deal with other ways than those of men. Yes, we are watched. And what will come of that watching I cannot say—"

But he did not answer me and I knew that no argument I could use would move him.

Within the maze of trees the path turned and twisted so much I lost all sense of direction. But I did not lose that thread which tied me to what I sought. And I knew this way would bring me there.

We came at last from under the shadow of the trees into moonlight. And there I saw what had been in the far-seeing—the spiral of pillars. They stood gleaming, ice-cold and frost-white, in the center of an open space.

I heard a sharp exclamation from Jervon and turned my head, startled. On his breast the loop cross had sprung to vivid fire, as if it had been fashioned not of moon-silver but of some huge gem. And I knew that what powered it had been awakened into the strongest life it could possess by the emanations from the spiral.

There was warmth also against my knee, and from the saddlebags came a dim radiance. I fumbled with the clasp, brought out the cup. There was left only a thin rim of silver undarkened—so little time had I left! But even that thread responded, too.

"Stay you here—" I gave that order. He might not obey it, but I must keep my mind on my own actions, think only of Elyn and what must be done to save him. Jervon had made his choice—on him be the result.

With the cup in one hand and in the other one of the things the Dame had pressed upon me, a wand of rowan peeled clean and then steeped in the potent juice of its own fruit, being after laid for the nights of the full moon exposed in a place of Old Power, I went forward. That was light enough weight, nothing compared to the sword which dragged at my hip. Yet I did not free myself of that, for it was wrought of metal which my mother and father had sought in strange places, so that in its way it was a talisman.

Thus with wand and cup, the knowledge that I alone could face what lay there, I stepped past the first pillar and began the winding path it marked.

# 6

## *Field of Stone*

THERE WAS a drawing at first, as if a current pulled at me, urging me on. Then came a sharp reversal. That which lurked here must have sensed that I came not bemused and ready as had its other victims. A pause, while I advanced steadily, cup and wand held as sword and shield ready for battle. Then—

What I had braced myself to meet from the beginning struck hard. It was like a blow, with force enough to stagger me. Yet it neither drove me to my knees nor into retreat. I had to fight as one might fight facing a buffeting storm wind.

Where I had gone easily and steadily before, now I wavered in spite of all my efforts, from side to side, winning only inches where I had taken strides. However, I schooled myself to think only of what I must do, put aside all uneasiness. For the least break which fear might make in my guard would leave me defenseless.

I held to one warming spark of hope. What I faced here was strong, yes, stronger than anything Aufrica and I had ever thrown skill and energy against, but it was not spun from the power of an adept. Part of its strength must be rooted in the fact that for a toll of years it had not been successfully withstood. Thus the very fact that I did battle was enough to slightly shake its belief in what it could and would do.

And I discovered that, though those pillars seemed to stand well apart from each other with space in between, there was a force field uniting them. So that once within the spiral one could not look out any more than one could through a wall. Also—

Almost I had been captured in the simplest of traps. I rated myself for my momentary inattention. I had been moving in a pattern, my attention so on the fact that I must keep moving that I was unaware my steps fitted the purposes of another, not my own. Straightaway I sought to break the lulling spell, stepping long, short, from side to side, even giving a small hop now and then, anything to keep from what might hypnotize mind and body.

I prepared for a new attack. Since that which awaited me had tried two ways, and both had failed, the third would be a greater threat.

The clear moonlight was gone. There was light, but it streamed from the pillars, as if each were the flame of some giant candle. That light was faintly green, giving an unpleasant look to the flesh of my hands, as if I were tainted with some foul disease.

But the wand and that section of the cup still unclouded were like twin torches in return, burning now with the blue of those safe candles which one uses in defensive spells.

Once more the assault began, and this time it was through sight. Things coiled, and glided, peered from between the flames of the pillars, showing faces and forms so foul as to be only of the Dark. My defense was not to be tempted to lift or turn my eyes from cup or wand.

To sight was added sound. There were voices I knew, which cried aloud to me, sometimes with pleas, sometimes sharp warnings. Having so beset sight and

hearing, the power in command here tried once more
to engulf me in the pattern of its weaving. Thus my
fight grew so that I was as a beleaguered swordsman
facing many foes at once, striving to keep them all
in play.

But my way was on and I kept to it.

Suddenly all sound, sight, pressure ceased. This was
withdrawal, not victory. The ruler of this place was
concentrating forces, waiting for me to reach the heart
of the spiral before loosing on me full power. I took
advantage of that release to push ahead faster.

I came into the heart of that net which had been
woven, or least put to the use of, she who had cursed
the Lords of Coomb Frome. And I moved into company. Men stood there, their faces all turned to the
center of the circle. Twelve of them I counted and
the last was Elyn!

In none of them was the spark of life. They were
like statues so perfectly fashioned that they needed
only breath and warmth to make them men, but both
they lacked. And all were bound by what they looked
upon.

There was a circular block raised in the center and
on it—

Mist thickened, became a form—that of a woman,
unclothed, beautiful. She raised her arms and tossed
high the wealth of her hair which was like a cloak,
but did not lie about her, rather rose in weaving ten-
drils, as if it had life of its own. Silver-white as moon-
shine was her body, silver hair her hair, only her eyes
were dark and seemed to have no whites, but were
like small pits far back in which something watched
the world with no good will.

She was perfect, she was beautiful, and there was
that in her, I recognized, to draw anything male to her.
It was as if the full essence of the female was distilled
and here given form and life.

So—me she did not draw—but repelled! For all which
makes one woman suspicious, or jealous, or brings her
to hate another, was also so distilled and brought to
the highest. And I do not think it was until that mo-

ment that she realized I was not what I outwardly appeared.

Her realization was followed by a blast of hate. But for that I was prepared, raising cup and wand before me swiftly. Her hair writhed wildly, reaching for me as if each strand fought to wreath itself noose-wise about my throat.

Then—she laughed.

There was scorn in that laughter. It was such as a queen might utter were the lowliest of her work-maids to challenge her power. So confident was she.

Her hands went to that flowing hair, and she broke away threads of it. As she held them they glittered even brighter, taking on the semblance of burnished metal. These she rolled and spun in her fingers to make a cord.

But I did not wait idly for her attack. What magic she was about to use I had heard of. It had a beginning as a love charm—and as such it might be considered relatively harmless. But the other face of love is hate, and in hate this could kill.

So I sang, not aloud, but in my head. And, as I watched her, my chant followed each and every turn and twist of her silver-bright fingers, bringing so a counter to what she did, as if I too wove a twin, though invisible, to her effort.

I could guess that what she did was far more potent than the charm I had knowledge of, she being who she was. But that she used a spell I could identify was a small tip of scales in my favor. I had come expecting the skill of a close-to-adept; I was faced with something known to every Wise Woman. Of course this might be only the first of many spells, which would grow in complexity and power as our struggle continued.

Now she had her loop, but she did not yet cast it, rather she passed it from hand to hand, those dark caverns of eyes ever upon me. I noted something else, that aura of the female, the sexual impact she had used as a weapon, was fading.

Her body was no longer of great and compelling

beauty, her limbs lengthened, grew thin and spare, her breasts flattened to her ribs, her face was a mask of bone covered thinly with skin. Only her hair remained the same.

But her lips stretched in a scornful smile. And for the first time she struck at me with words. Though whether she spoke them aloud or from mind to mind I did not know.

"Witch one—look at me and see yourself. This is how you look to others!"

If she thought to catch me through vanity— Had she so poor an idea of human women that she believed such a small assault would win her any even temporary victory?

Her words meant nothing. It was the noose to which I must pay attention.

"What man follows such as you—" Her taunting stopped. Her head went up, her eyes no longer strove to hold mine, even her hands were still, the noose of hair hanging limply from one. Her attitude was one of listening. Yet I could hear nothing.

Once more a change came over her, beauty flowed back to round her body, make her the idealized image of what any man would joyfully claim as a bed-fellow. Again she laughed.

"Witch, I have underrated you. It seems you do have one willing to follow where you led. But what a pity—from a beggar even his bowl shall be taken. Watch, Witch, and see how works the power of—" Then she shook her head and my heart warmed. For I realized how nearly she had been off guard, almost she had said her name. And, if she had uttered that, she would have truly lost. It had been so long since she had faced any kind of opposition that she was careless. Therefore I must be ever alert, ready to take advantage of any such slip.

"Turn and look, Witch," she urged. "See who comes now at my calling, as did all of these fools!"

I did not need to do so, nor would I lower my guard. If Jervon had come, then he must take the consequences. I could not let myself be shaken in any way from the battle between the silver woman and me.

I heard rather than saw him move into place beside me. Then his hand came into my line of vision and I saw he had drawn his sword, was holding it point out to the woman.

She began to sing, a sweet beguiling. And she held out her hands to him, though she had not dropped the noose. And in her, woman that I was, I could see all the enticement my sex might ever hold for a man, promising him every delight of body.

Jervon moved forward.

Nor could I lay any blame on him, for this was sorcery which even the blazing loop cross at his throat could not avert. It was too distilled, too potent—

And that potency awakened in me the same anger which I had felt before, as if the silver woman threatened all I could ever hold dear. Still I was a Wise Woman and to such the body and emotions must ever be controlled by the mind.

She was speaking, a flow of crooning, compelling words—aimed at Jervon. I saw the sword waver, the point sink to the ground. His other hand went to paw at the loop cross, pull at it as if he would break the chain and throw that talisman from him. But also I sensed something else.

Strong was her spell, yes. But he was fighting it. Not in fear, as the others might have fought when they came to realize the deadly enticement they faced, but because he knew in some part of him that this was not truly his desire.

How this came to me I do not know, perhaps because it struck at her also. Her arms reached, she was desire incarnate—waiting for him alone. His hand was on the loop cross, no longer pulling at it, no, rather clutching as if that gave him safe anchorage in the midst of a storm.

What I had been waiting for happened; the noose spun out through the air. But not aimed for me—at Jervon, as if his stubborn refusal to surrender had again shaken her from careful planning.

I was waiting, the tip of the wand catching into that loop. Straightaway it curled itself around the peeled branch as it would have around flesh had it touched. But as swiftly it released that hold, made to slip down to my hand.

I shook the wand, saw those coils loosen, and the noose was sent flying back toward her who had sent it. It landed at the foot of the block on which she stood and humped into life like a serpent, began to crawl back again toward us. But the silver woman was already weaving another such from her hair, plaiting it with flying fingers this time, not leisurely as she had before.

Jervon only stood, his hand still on the hilt of his sword which now rested point against the pavement, the other clasped over the loop cross. I knew that he could not defend himself more than he did at present, resisting her spell. I would have to meet her attacks alone. But at greater disadvantage than before for she could take Jervon unless I divided my defense.

Dared I do that? I wavered, and then was angered by my own wavering. In this I had no choice. If Jervon was to fall to her sorcery, that I must allow, keeping single-minded on the last struggle between the two of us.

Once more she had a noose, but this time she did not fling it at either of us, rather dropped it lightly to the pavement where, as its fellow, it began to wriggle toward us. She was smiling again, already weaving a third while the two others humped and crawled.

Yes, this was such an attack as might win for her—might— But I clung to the doubt. I thrust the cup into the fore of my belt, and with my left hand drew the sword my father had forged from the lumps of ancient metal.

It caught no reflection from the light around us. The whole of the blade was dark, thickly dark as a night without moon or stars. Never had I seen it so before; always it had been as any other weapon. But it might now have been forged from shadows.

I laid it on the pavement before me, edge toward

the creeping nooses. What protection it might give I did not know. There are powers which can be defeated by metals, even other powers which feed upon them. But this was strangely wrought and I had belief in the judgment of my parents who had valued it so highly.

Once more I took the cup into my hand, waited with it and the wand. But I had to divide my attention now between the actions of the woman and the crawling nooses—three of them—for she had finished that and was busy with a fourth.

One of the nooses reached close to the blade I had laid down. It coiled back upon itself, as might a serpent preparing to strike, one end raised from the ground, darting back and forth as if it were before a wall it could not pierce or climb. For the moment I had the relief of knowing I had another defense.

To my surprise Jervon moved, heavily and jerkily as one who fights the dead weight of his own body, but he brought up his sword, slashed at the coiled noose. It struck back at his blade, strove to wind about it, yet fell away. So steel was also a defense.

Those who stood statue-still about us were mainly armed, but their blades were all sheathed. Perhaps they had been so ensorceled that they had not been aware that they must fight for freedom.

The silver woman hissed like a great enraged cat. She hurled her fourth noose at me and once more the wand caught it, threw it back. But at that moment I knew that I must not leave her the initiative.

I poised the wand as I might a hunting spear, hurled it straight for her breast. She gave a loud keening cry and swept her hair out as a shield.

I saw the wand thrust deep into that and the strands melted back and away. But she had deflected the wand and it clattered down against the block on which she stood and broke. Yet half her hair was shriveled away.

Quickly I caught up the sword at my feet. And Jervon, still moving as if leaden weights were fastened to his arms, was striking awkwardly at the remaining

67

nooses. But he moved so slowly they could well take him first.

There was no time to consider Jervon. I must think only of what was to be done here and now. I leaped over the crawling nooses, straight for that block on which she stood tearing at her hair, not waiting to weave cords but throwing handfuls of it at us both, it flowing in cloudy masses through the air.

I waved the sword back and forth before me to clear that menace. Then I stood before her. Her face was no longer beautiful. Once more she showed a skull countenance. Her lips were drawn back against her teeth; her hands, ceasing to comb at her hair, were outstretched. Before my eyes they became huge talons reaching to rend and tear.

I readied the sword, thrusting up and in. And met nothing. Yet still she stood there ready to launch herself at my throat. Again I thrust. Then I knew—what I saw was illusion; the core of it lay elsewhere. And I must find that or lose the battle entirely.

There was a thin cry. Jervon had slashed two nooses, the third had fastened on his foot, was weaving up his body. But I had no time— I must find the witch core.

That it lay somewhere in this spiral heart I could not doubt. She could not have manifested so strongly otherwise.

The woman did not move from where she stood, though her claw hands were still outstretched, her head turned at what seemed an impossible angle on her shoulders so she could follow me with those eyes which were not eyes. With her mouth pulled into a furious snarl, she lost more and more of her human aspect, her rage mirrored in her body.

I realized now that she was tied to the block and could do no more than her hair tricks and the like. As long as I was alert for such moves, I was free to seek that which must be found if she were to be wholly destroyed or driven away.

Passing among those silent figures of her victims I reached the pillars about that core. I moved along them slowly, checking ever upon the movements of the enemy.

She raised her hand to her face, those claws melted again into fingers, and she cupped them together as if she sheltered some precious thing. Then she brought her hands to her mouth, blew gently into them as if she had need for warmth.

But I knew that what she so blew was a new way of attack, though I could not guess its manner. Suddenly she spread her hands wide, and crouched between them was a small thing the like of which I had never seen before, save I knew it to be evil.

Wings which were flaps of mottled skin it had, and a horned head, and a sharply pointed snout. It was as red as a leaping fire spark. And like the menace of wind-driven flame, it was as she tossed it aloft. I expected it to strike at me, but rather it winged up and up, vanishing quickly.

I did not know from which direction it might return, or when. Yet I dared not linger to wait on it, I must continue my search. So I kept on from pillar to pillar. And ever she watched me, her teeth like fangs, her grin that of death itself.

Since the wand was shattered, I pinned my hopes on the cup. A thing of power, it must react to power when it neared the source which fed the apparition of the woman. Yet the small silver portion grew no brighter.

By then I had made the circuit of the pillars. So— the obvious must be true. The source lay under that block on which she stood. But how to force it up or off—

I came up behind Jervon. His legs were now netted by not only the third noose but some of the flying hair she had sent against us. None rose high up his body and his sword arm was still free. It would take the two of us—I knew that now. But could he—would he —aid?

I passed my black sword up and about him. The nets shriveled into nothingness. He turned his head. His

69

face was set, white, with some of the rigid look of those others. But his eyes were alive.

"You must help—with that stone—"

I laid the sword tip to his shoulder. He shuddered, moved stiffly.

Yet all the time I remembered that winged scarlet thing she had sent flying. Was it poised for attack somewhere over our heads, or was it a messenger to summon aid for her?

Jervon took one ponderous step and then another at my urging. He moved so slowly it was as if stone itself obeyed my wishes. I put the cup again into my belt, caught his wrist, and set the point of his sword at the jointure of stone and pavement.

An arm with misshapen talons raked inches short of his face, yet something, perhaps the loop cross, kept him safe. I went to set my sword point even with his and I cried out—hoping with all my might he could do as I ordered:

"Heave!"

Both hands I had set about the hilt of the sword. And at that moment came the scarlet flying thing, aiming for my eyes. I jerked my head, but by the favor of those powers I had long served, I did not lose my grip.

Like a brand of fire along my cheek was that stinging blow. I could hear a hissing whine. But all that mattered, all that must matter was the stone. And it was moving!

I put forth all my strength, at the same time crying again:

"Jervon, heave!"

And that stone, under the urging of our blades, arose up, though the flying thing darted about our heads and I heard Jervon cry out, saw him stagger back. But we had done it—the stone was up, poised on one edge for an instant, then crashed over and away.

# 7

## *Silver Bright*

SHE WHO HAD menaced us from the block was gone. But the red flyer darted again at my eyes in such a fury of attack that I stumbled away half-blinded. In my hand was still the sword, and I thrust with it down into whatever we might have uncovered. There was a low wail. The red thing vanished.

I stood at the edge of a small pit. There had been a casket there in the hollow but the point of the sword had pierced it, cleaving the metal as if it were no more than soft earth. From that now spread a melting so that the riven casket lost shape, became a mass, which in turn sank into the ground on which it lay. In moments nothing was left.

Now the very pavement under my feet began to crack and crumble in turn, becoming rubble. First around the edges of the pit, and then, that erosion spreading, in lapping waves, as if all the untold years that this place had had its existence settled all at once, a burden of age too heavy to support.

The waves of erosion touched the feet of the first man. He shivered, moved. Then his armor was rust red, holding bare bones, until all toppled, to crash in shards, bone and time-eaten iron together, to the riven pavement.

So it was with the rest. Dead men, losing the false semblance of life as time caught up and engulfed them, to reach to the next and the next.

"Dead!" Jervon said.

I looked around. He had lost that rigid cast of countenance, was staring about him as if he wakened from some half-stupor into full consciousness.

"Yes, dead, long dead. As is this trap now."

I pulled my sword from the pit where it had been standing upright, its point no longer anchored in the

71

box, but in the dark ground. But that point—it was eroded, as if it had been thrust into acid. I held but three-quarters of a weapon. I sheathed it, amazed at what power must have erupted from the box.

Elyn! Almost I had forgotten him who had brought me hither.

Swinging from that hole I looked to where my brother stood, one among the other prisoners. He moved, raised a hand uncertainly to his head, tried to take a step and tripped over the bones and armor of one of his less fortunate fellows. I sped to him, my hands ready to steady him. He was blinking, looking about as one who wakes out of a dream, to perhaps find not all of it a dream after all.

"Elyn!" I shook him gently as one shakes awake a child who had cried out of a nightmare.

He looked at me slowly.

"Elys?" But of my name he made a question, as if he did not believe I was real.

"Elys," I assured him. And, though I still kept one hand upon his arm, I held out now the cup.

That dark tarnish was gone. And in the moonlight the silver was as bright as it had been from the night it was first wrought. He put out his hand, traced the rim with one finger.

"Dragon scale silver—"

"Yes. It told me that you were in danger—brought me here—"

With that he looked up and around. The erosion had spread. Those pillars had lost their eerie light; most of them had crumbled and fallen away. The power which had knitted it all together had fled.

"Where—where is this place?" Elyn was frowning, puzzled. And I wondered if he knew at all what had happened to him.

"This is the heart of Ingaret's Curse. And you were caught in it—"

"Ingaret!" That single name seemed to be enough. "Brunissende—where is my lady?"

"Safe in the Keep at Coomb Frome." But there was an odd feeling in me. It was as if Elyn had taken a step away from me—a step? No, a stride—still my hand was on him.

"I do not remember—" Some of his uncertainty returned.

"That does not matter. You are free."

"We are all free, Lady. But are we like to remain so?"

Jervon was by me. He still held his unsheathed sword and he had the watchfulness of one who treads through enemy territory where each wayside bush may mask armed surprise.

"The power here is gone." I was sure of that.

"But is it the only power hereabouts? I shall feel safer when we are to horse and on the back trail."

"Who is this?" Elyn spoke to me.

I thought perhaps some of the mind daze still held by his curt question, and I made ready answer.

"This is Jervon, Marshal of Haverdale, who has ridden with me for your deliverance. It was by his sword aid that we won this battle with the Curse."

"I give thanks," Elyn said remotely.

I thought—he is still under the edge of the spell, his wits are slowed, so I can forgive his bareness of thanks. Yet his manner chilled me a little.

"Coomb Frome—where lies it?" At least on that question Elyn's voice was alive and eager.

"A day's ride away," Jervon answered.

In that moment I could not have said anything, for it was as if the struggle with the silver woman had sustained me against any weariness, but now that that was past, and Elyn once more free, all fatigue settled upon me at once, as time had done to crack open this foul web. I staggered. Instantly there was an arm at my back, strong as any keep wall, supporting me.

"Let us ride then!" Elyn was already starting away.

"Presently." Jervon's word had the crack of an order. "Your lady sister has ridden through one day without rest, battled through the night, to win you free. She cannot ride now."

Elyn glanced impatiently around, a stubborn look I knew of old on his face.

73

"I—" he began, and then after a moment's pause, he nodded. "Well enough."

If he said that grudgingly, I was far too sunk in this vast weariness to care. Nor was I really aware of how we came free of the ruins of the spiral. Or of aught, save a drowsy memory of resting on the ground, with the soft roll of a cloak beneath my head, my furred one spread over me, while a firm hand held mine and a far-off voice urged me to sleep.

I awoke to the tantalizing fragrance of roasting meat, saw through half-open eyes the dancing flames of a fire, and near that, on spits of branches, the bodies of forest fowl, small but of such fine eating that not even a Dale lord would disdain to find one on his feast table.

Jervon, his helm laid aside, the ringed-under hood of that lying back on his shoulders, sat cross-legged, watching the roasting birds with a critical eye. Elyn—? I turned my head slowly, but my brother was not to be seen in the firelight, and I levered myself up, his name a cry on my lips.

Jervon swung around and came to me quickly.

"Elyn?" I cried again.

"Is safe. He rode out at noontide, being anxious concerning his wife, and doubtless his command."

I had shaken sleep from me now, and there was that in the tone of his voice which made me uneasy.

"But dangerous country—you said yourself to ride alone across it was deep peril—with three of us—" I was babbling, I realized, but there was something here I could not understand.

"He is a man, full armed. He chose to go. Would you have had me overpower and bind him into staying?" Still that note in his voice.

"I do not understand—" My confusion grew.

Jervon arose abruptly, half turned from me to face the fire, yet still I could see the flat plane of his cheek, the firmness of his chin, that straight line which his mouth assumed upon occasion.

"Nor do I!" There was heat in his voice now. "Had any wrought for me as you did for him—then I would not have left her side. Yet all he pratted of was his lady! If he thought so much of her, how came he into the toils of that—?"

"He perhaps cannot remember." I pushed aside the furred cloak. "Oftentimes ensorcelment has that effect upon the victim. And once that power set up its lure he could not have resisted. You remember surely what spell she cast. Had you not the loop cross it might so have drawn you."

"Well enough!" But his voice did not lose that heat. "Perhaps he acted as any man. Save, that from *your* brother one does not expect the act of any man. And—" he hesitated as if he chewed upon some words he did not want to say yet there was that forcing him to the saying, "Lady, do not expect— Oh, what matter it. I may be seeing drawn swords where all are sheathed. What say you to food?"

I wanted to know what chafed in his mind, but I would not force it from him. And hunger was greater than all now. Eagerly I reached for a spitted bird, blew upon it and my fingers as I strove to strip the browned flesh from its small bones.

So long had I slept that it was dawn about us when we finished that meal. Jervon brought up the single horse. So Elyn had taken the other! That had not occurred to me. My brother's behavior seemed more strange as I thought on it.

I did not gainsay Jervon when he insisted that I ride. But I made up my mind that I would not spend the whole of this journey in the saddle; like true comrades, we would share alike.

However, as we went, my thoughts were well occupied with Elyn. Not just that he had left us so—any man newly out of a spell might well be so overcast in his mind to hold only to one desire and the need for obtaining it. If Brunissende meant so much to him, he might see in her the safety he craved. No, I could not count his leaving as unfeeling, for I had never been in the grip of a spell.

It was Elyn the boy I began to remember, recalling all I had once accepted without question. Though why

I had this overshadowing feeling that I was about to face another testing I could not tell. Save that no one who had Wise Learning ever puts aside such uneasiness as without cause.

Elyn had never shown any interest in the Wise Way. In fact, now that I faced memories squarely and sounded them for full meaning, he had shunned that. Though I had had laid on me the vows of silence in many things, there had been lesser bits of learning he might well have profited by. Also he had not liked it when I had shown my arts in his presence.

Oddly enough he had not resented the fact that I shared his swordplay. He had treated me then more as a brother, and I had been content. But let me speak of what I might do with Aufrica and he had shied away. Yet at that last meeting he had allowed the cup pledge. The first time, to my knowledge, that he had ever agreed to any spell binding.

We both knew our mother's story, that she had sought out powers which might prove fatal in order to give our father a son. She had forged the dragon cup—but at the last moment she had asked for a daughter also, gladly paying with her life.

So we had not been conceived as ordinary children; magic had played a part in our lives from the beginning. Did Elyn fear because of this?

Though I had been much with him and my father, yet I had had those other hours of which my father never spoke. He, too, as I recalled those years now, had seemed to ignore that side of my life. As if it were something—like—like a deformity!

I drew a deep breath, a whole new conception of my past opening before me. Had my father and Elyn felt aversion—even shame— But how could they? There was my mother— What had happened in that land of Estcarp across the sea which had rift my parents from their former life, tossed them into barren Wark?

Shame of the power? Did my father, my brother, look upon me as one marked—or tainted—?

"No!" I denied that aloud.

"No what, my lady?"

Startled, I looked at Jervon walking beside me. I hesitated then. There was a question I longed to ask, yet shrank from the asking. Then I nerved myself to it, for by the reply I might perhaps find some solution to the problem of Elyn.

"Jervon, do you know what I am?" I asked it baldly, my voice perhaps a little hoarse as I braced myself for his answer.

"A very gallant lady—and a mistress of powers," he replied.

"Yes, a Wise Woman." I would not have flattery from him. "One who deals with the unseen."

"To some good purpose, as you have here. What troubles you, Lady?"

"I do not believe that all men think as you do, comrade. That there is good in being a mistress of powers. Or if they admit so much at times, they are not always so charitable. I was bred up to such knowledge, to me it is life. I cannot imagine being without—though it walls me from others. There are those who always look askance at me."

"Including Elyn?"

He was quick, too quick. Or perhaps I was stupid enough to give away my thoughts. But since I had gone this far, why try to conceal my misgivings farther?

"Perhaps—I do not know."

Had I hoped he would deny that? If so, I was disappointed, for after a moment his reply came:

"If that is the way with him, it could explain much. And having been caught in what he distrusted—yes, he could wish to see the last of all which would remind him—"

I reined in the horse. "But it is not so with you?"

Jervon put his hand to sword hilt. "This is my defense, my weapon. It is steel and I can touch it, all men can see it in my hand. But there are other weapons, as you have so ably proved. Should I fear, or look sidewise (as you say) upon them because they are not metal, or perhaps not visible? Learning in the arts of war I have, and also, once, some in the ways of peace. That came to me by study. You have yours by study also. I may not understand it, but perhaps there is that in my learning also which would be strange to you. Why should one learning be less or more than any other when they are from different sources? You have healcraft which is your peace art, and what you have done to lay this Curse is your art of war.

"No, I do not look with fear—or aversion—on what you do."

So did he answer the darkest of my thoughts.

But if I must accept that Elyn felt differently, what lay in days ahead? I could return to that nameless dale—unless early winter sealed it off—where the Wark folk stayed. There was nothing to tie me to them save Aufrica. Yet I had known when I rode forth that her farewell to me had been lasting. There was no need for two Wise Women there, and she had done her best for me. I was now a woman grown and proven in power. The hatched fledgling cannot be refitted into the eggshell from which it has broken free.

Coomb Frome? No, I had nothing there either. I was sure I had read Brunissende right in the short time I had seen her. She might accept her Dame, but a Wise Woman close kin to her lord—there would be more sidewise looks.

But if I went not to the Dale nor to the Keep, where would I venture? Now I looked about me wonderingly, for it seemed, in that moment of realization, I was indeed cast adrift and even the land around me took on a more forbidding cast.

"Do we go on?" Once more Jervon spoke as if he could read my unhappy thoughts.

"Where else is there to go?" For the first time in our companying I looked to him for an answer, having none myself.

"I would say not the Keep!" The decision in that was sharp and clear. "Or, if you wish, only to make sure of Elyn's return, to visit only and let that visit be brief."

I seized upon that—it would give me breathing space, a time to think—to plan.

"To Coomb Frome then—in brief."

Though we perforce went slowly, by midafternoon we were sighted by those Elyn had sent to meet us. So I came a second time to the Keep. I noted also that, though we were treated with deference by that party, yet Elyn had not ridden with them.

We reached the Keep long after moonrise and I was shown into a guest chamber where serving maids waited with a steaming copper of water to ease the aches of travel, a bed such as I had never known for softness. But I had slept far better the night before on the bare ground in the wilderness, for my thoughts pricked and pulled at me.

In the morn I arose and the maids brought me a soft robe such as the Dale ladies wore. But I asked for my mailed shirt and travel clothes. They were then in a fluster so I learned that by my Lady Brunissende's own orders those clothes had been destroyed as too travel-worn.

Under my urging one of the maids bethought herself of other clothing and brought it to me. Man's it was but new. Whether it had been for my brother, I knew not. But I wore it together with boots, my mail, and the sword belt and sheath in which rested the mutilated weapon which had routed the Curse.

I left my cloak, my saddlebags, and journey wallet in my room. My brother, they told me, was still with his lady—and I sent to ask for a meeting.

So I went for the second time into that fated tower room. Brunissende saw me first and she gasped, put out her hand to grasp tight Elyn's silken sleeve. For he wore no armor.

He gazed at me with a growing frown. Then he took her hand gently from his arm to stride towards me, his frown heavy as he looked me up and down.

"Why come you here in such guise, Elys? Can you not understand that to see you so is difficult for Brunissende?"

"To see me so? I have been so all my life, brother. Or have you forgotten—?"

"I have forgotten nothing!" he burst out, and it was as if he were deliberately feeding his anger, if anger

79

it was, that he might brace himself to harsh words. "What was done in Wark is long past. You have to forget those rough ways. My dear lady will aid you to do so."

"Will she now? And I have much to forget, do I, brother? It would seem you have already forgotten!"

His hand came up; I think he was almost moved to strike me. And I realized that he feared most of all—not me as a Wise Woman, but that I might make plain to Brunissende the manner of his ensorcelment.

"It is forgotten—" He said those words as a warning.

"So be it." I had had no decision to make after all. It had been made for me, days, seasons—long ago. We might be of one birth, of one face, but we were otherwise hardly kin. "I ask nothing of you, Elyn, save a horse. Since I do not propose to travel afoot—and that I think you owe me."

His frown cleared a little. "Where do you go? Back to those of Wark?"

I shrugged but did not answer. If he wished to believe that, let him. I was still amazed at the chasm between us.

"You are wise." Brunissende had crept to his side. "Men hereabouts still fear the Curse. That you have had dealings with that power seems fearsome to them."

Elyn stirred. "She broke it for me. Never forget that, my lady."

She answered nothing to that, only eyed me in such a way as I knew there could be no friendship between us.

"The day grows, I will ride." I had no desire to prolong this viewing of something already buried in the past.

He gave me the best mount in his stable, ordered out also a pack horse and had it loaded with gear. I did not deny him this attempt to salve his conscience. All the time I saw the looks of his men who, seeing us so like together, must have longed for the mystery to be explained.

After I had mounted I looked down at him. I did not want to wish him ill. He lived by his nature, I

80

mine. Instead I made a sign to summon fortune and blessing to him. And saw his mouth tighten as if he wanted it not.

So I rode from Coomb Frome, but at the gate another joined me. And I said:

"Have you learned where your lord now lies? Which way do you ride to return to his standard?"

"He is dead. The men of his following—those still living—enlisted under other banners. I am without a lord."

"Then where do you go, swordsman?"

"I am without a lord, but I have found a lady. Your road is mine, mistress of powers."

"Well enough. But which road and where?"

"There is still a war, Lady. I have my sword and you yours. Let us seek where we can best harry the Hounds!"

I laughed. I had turned my back on Coomb Frome. I was free—for the first time I was free—of Aufrica's governing, of the wretched survivors of Wark, of the spell of the dragon cup, which henceforth would be only a cup and not any lodestone to draw me into danger. Unless—I glanced at Jervon, but he was not looking at me, but eagerly at the road ahead—unless, I chose to make it otherwise. Which at some future day I might just do.

# DREAM SMITH

THERE ARE MANY TALES which the song-
smiths beat out in burnished telling, some old and some
new. And the truth of this one or that—who knows?
Yet at the heart of the most improbable tale may lie
a kernel of truth. So it was with the tale of the Dream
Smith—though for any man now living to prove it—
he might as well try to empty Fos Tern with a kitch-
en ladle!

Broson was smith in Ghyll, having both the greater
and the smaller mysteries of that craft. Which is to
say that he wrought in bronze and iron and also in
precious metals. Though the times he could use tools
on the latter were few and far between.

He had two sons, Arnar and Collard. Both were, in
boyhood, deemed likely youths, so that Broson was
looked upon, not only in Ghyll (which lies at river-
fork in Ithondale), but as far off as Sym and Boldre,
as a man well fortuned. Twice a year he traveled by
river to Twyford with small wear of his own making,
wrought hinges and sword blades, and sometimes
brooches and necklets of hill silver.

This was in the days before the invaders came and
High Hallack was at peace, save with outlaws, woods-
runners, and the like, who raided now and then from
the wastes. Thus it was needful that men in the upper
dales have weapons to hand.

Vescys was lord in Ithondale. But the Dalesmen saw
little of him since he heired, through his mother, holdings in the shorelands and there married a wife with
more. So only a handful of elderly men and a wash-
wife or two were at the Keep and much of it was
closed from winter's midfeast to the next.

It was in the third year after Vescys' second marriage (the Dalesmen having that proclaimed to them

by a messenger) that something of more import to Ghyll itself occurred.

A trader came down from the hills, one of his ponies heavily laden with lumps of what seemed pure metal, yet none Broson could lay name to. It had a sheen, even unworked, which fascinated the smith. And, having tried a small portion by fire and hammer, he enthusiastically bargained for the whole of the load. Though the peddler was evasive when asked to name the source, Broson decided that the man was trying to keep secret something which might well bring him profit again. Since the pony was lame, the man consented with visible (or so it appeared) reluctance to sell, leaving in one of Broson's metal bins two sacks of what was more melted scrap than ore.

Broson did not try to work it at once. Rather he spent time studying, thinking out how best he might use it. His final decision was to try first a sword. It was rumored that Lord Vescys might visit this most western of his holdings, and to present his lord with such an example of smith work could only lead to future favor.

The smelting Broson gave over to Collard, since the boy was well able to handle such a matter. He had determined that each of his sons in turn would learn to work with this stuff, always supposing that the peddler would return, as Broson was sure he would, with a second load.

And in that he gave his son death-in-life, even as he had once given him life.

For, though no man could ever learn what had gone wrong in the doing, for all those standing by, including Broson himself, had detected no carelessness on Collard's part (he was known to be steady and painstaking), there was an explosion which nigh burst the smithy to bits.

There were burns and hurts, but Collard had taken the worst of both. It would have been better had he died in that moment. For when he dragged back into half-life after weary months of torment and despair, he was no longer a man.

Sharvana, Wise Woman and healer, took the broken body into her keeping. What crawled out of her house was no Collard, a straight, upstanding son for any man to eye with pride, but a thing such as you see sometimes carved (luckily much weathered away) on the ruins left by the Old Ones.

Not only was his body so twisted that he walked bent over like a man on whom hundreds of seasons weighed, but his face was a mask such as might leer at the night from between trees of a haunted forest. Sharvana had an answer to that, but it was not enough to shield him entirely from the eyes of his fellows—though all were quick to avert their gaze when he shambled by.

She took supple bark and made a mask to hide his riven face. And that he wore at all times. But still he kept well out of the sight of all.

Nor did he return to his father's house, but rather took an old hut at the foot of the garden. This he worked upon at night, never coming forth by day lest his old comrades might sight him. And he rebuilt it into a snug enough shelter. For, while the accident seemed to have blasted all else, it had not destroyed his clever hands, nor the mind behind the ruined face.

He would work at the forge at night, but at last Broson said no to that. For there was objection to the sound of hammers, and the people of Ghyll wanted no reminding of who used them. So Collard came no more to the smithy.

What he did no man knew, and he came to be almost forgotten. The next summer, when his brother married Nicala of the Mill, he never appeared at the wedding, nor ventured out in those parts of the yard and garden where those of the household might see him.

It was in the third year after his accident that Collard did come forward, and only because another peddler came into the forge. While the trader was dickering with Broson, Collard stood in the shadows. But when the bargain for a set of belt knives was settled, the smith's son lurched forward to touch the trader's arm.

He did not speak, but motioned to a side table whereon he had spread out a square of cloth and set up a series of small figures. They were fantastical in form, some animals, some men, but such men as might be heroes from the old tales, so perfect were their bodies. As if poor Collard, doomed to go crooked for as long as he lived, had put into these all his longing to be one with his fellows.

Some were of wood, but the greater number of metal. Broson, astounded at viewing such, noted the sheen of the metal. It was the strange stuff he had thrown aside, fearing to handle again after the accident.

The trader saw their value at once and made an offer. But Collard, with harsh croaks of voice, brought about what even Broson thought a fair bargain.

When the man had gone Broson turned eagerly to his son. He even forgot the strangeness of that blank mask which had only eyes to give it the semblance of a living man.

"Collard, how made you these? I have never seen such work. Even in Twyford, in the booths of merchants from overseas— Before—before you never fashioned such." Looking at that mask his words began to falter. It was as if he spoke not to his son, but to something as alien and strange as those beings reputed to dance about certain stones at seasons of the year, stones prudent men did not approach.

"I do not know—" came the grating voice, hardly above an animal's throaty growl. "They come into my head—then I make them."

He was turning away when his father caught at his arm. "Your trade—"

There were coins from overseas, good for exchange or for metal, a length of crimson cloth, two knife handles of carven horn.

"Keep it." Collard might be trying to shrug but his convulsive movement sent him off balance, so he must clutch at the tabletop. "What need has such as I to lay up treasure? I have no bride price to bargain for."

"But if you wanted not what the trader had to offer—why this?" Arnar, who had been watching, demanded. He was a little irked that his brother, who
was younger and, in the old days had no great promise, could suddenly produce such marketable wares.

"I do not know." Again Collard slewed around, this
time turning his bark mask in his brother's direction.
"I think I wished to know if they had value enough
to attract a shrewd dealer. But, yes, father, you have
reminded me of another debt." He took up the length
of fine cloth, a small gold coin which had been looped
so that one might wear it on a neck chain. "The Wise
Woman served me as best she could."

He then added: "For the rest—let it be for my share
of the household, since I cannot earn my bread at the
forge."

At dusk he carried his offering to Sharvana. She
watched as he laid coin and cloth on the table in her
small house, so aromatic of drying herbs and the brews
from them. An owl with a wing in splints perched on
a shelf above his head, and other small wild things, here
tame, had scuttled into cover at his coming.

"I have it ready—" She went to the cupboard, bringing out another mask. This was even more supple. He
fingered it wonderingly.

"Well-worked parchment," she told him, "weather-
treated, too. I have been searching for something to
suit your purpose. Try it. You have been at work?"

He took from the safe pocket of his jerkin the last
thing he had brought her. If the trader had coveted
what he had seen that morn, how much more he would
have wanted this. It was a figure of a winged woman,
her arms wide and up as if she were about to take to
the skies in search of something there seen and greatly
desired. For this was to the figures he had sold as a
finished sword blade is to the first rough casting.

"You have seen—*her?*" Sharvana put out her hand
as if to gather up the figure, but she did not quite touch
it.

"As the rest," he grated. "The dreams—then I awaken.
And I find that, after a fashion, I can make the dream

89

people. Wise Woman, if you were truly friend to me, you would give me from your stores that which would make me dream and never wake again!"

"That I cannot do, as you know. The virtue of my healing would then pour away, like running water, through my fingers. But you know not why you dream, or of what places?" Her voice became eager, as if she had some need to learn this.

"I know only that the land I see is not the Dales— at least the Dales as they now are. Can a man dream of the far past?"

"A man dreams of his own past. Why not, were the gift given, of a past beyond his own reckoning?"

"Gift!" Collard caught up that one word and made it an oath. "What *gift—?*"

She looked from him to the winged figure. "Collard, were you ever able to make such before?"

"You know not. But to see my hands so—I would trade all for a straight back and a face which would not afright a woman into screaming!"

"You have never let me foresee for you—"

"No! Nor shall I!" he burst out. "Who would want that if he were as I am now? As to why this—this dreaming and the aftermaking of my dream people has come upon me—well, that which I was handling in the smithy was no common metal. There must have been some dire ensorcelment in it. That trader never returned so we could ask about it."

"It is my belief," said Sharvana, "that it came from some stronghold of the Old Ones. They had their wars once, only the weapons used were no swords, nor spears, no crossbow darts, but greater. It could be that trader ventured into some old stronghold and brought forth the remains of such weapons."

"What matter?" asked Collard.

"Only this—things which a man uses with emotion, fashions with his hands, carries with him, draw into themselves a kind of—I can only call it 'life.' This holds though many seasons may pass. And if that remnant of emotion, that life, is suddenly released—it could well pass in turn into one unwary, open—"

90

"I see." Collard ran fingertips across the well-scrubbed surface of the table. "Then as I lay hurt I was so open —and there entered into me perhaps the memories of other men?"

She nodded eagerly. "Just so! Perhaps you see in dreams the Dales as they were before the coming of our people."

"And what good is that to me?"

"I do not know. But use it, Collard, use it! For if a gift goes unused it withers and the world is the poorer for it."

"The world?" his croak was far from laughter. "Well enough, I can trade these. And if I earn my bread so, then no man need trouble me. It is young to learn that all one's life must be spent walking a dark road, turning never into any welcoming door along the way."

Sharvana was silent. Suddenly she put out her hand, caught his before he could draw back, turning it palm-up in the lamplight.

He would have jerked free if he could, but in that moment her strength was as great as that of any laboring smith, and she had him pinned. Now she leaned forward to study the lines on the flesh so exposed.

"No foreseeing!" He cried that. The owl stirred and lifted its sound wing.

"Am I telling you?" she asked. "Have it as you wish, Collard. I have said naught." She released his wrist.

He was uneasy, drawing back his hand quickly, rubbing the fingers of the other about that wrist as if he would erase some mark she had left there.

"I must be going." He caught up the parchment mask—that he would try on only in his own hut where none could see his face between the taking off of one covering and the putting on of another.

"Go with the good will of the house." Sharvana used the farewell of their people. But somehow those words eased his spirit a little.

Time passed. All avoided Collard's hut, he invited no visitors, not even his father. Nor did another trader come. Instead there was news from the greater world

outside the Dale, a world which seemed to those of
Ghyll that of a songsmith.

When the Lord Vescys had wedded, his second wife
had had already a daughter, though few had heard of
her. But now the story spread throughout all of Ghyll
and to the out-farms and steads beyond.

For a party had ridden to the Keep, and thereafter
there was much cleaning and ordering of the rooms
in the mid-tower. It was that Vescys was sending his
daughter, the Lady Jacinda, to the country, for she
sickened in the town.

"Sickened!" Collard, on his way to the well, paused
in the dark, for the voice of his sister-in-law Nicala
was sharp and ringing in the soft dusk. "This is no new
thing. When Dame Matild had me come into the rooms
to see how much new herb rushing was needed for
the undercarpeting, she spoke freely enough. The young
lady has never been better than she is now—a small,
twisted thing, looking like a child, not a maid of years
like to wed. Not that our lord will ever find one to
bed with her unless he sweetens the bargain with such
dowry as even a High Lord's daughter could bring!

"The truth of it is, as Dame Matild said—the new
Lady Gwennan, she wants not this daughter near her.
Very delicate she is, and says she cannot bear my
lord a straight son if she sees even in bower and at
table such a twisted, crooked body."

Collard set his pail noiselessly down and moved a
step or two nearer the window. For the first time in
seasons curiosity stirred in him. He willed Nicala to
continue.

Which she did, though he gained little more facts.
Until Broson growled he wanted his mulled ale, and
she went to clatter at the hearth. Collard, once more
in his hut, did not reach for his tools, but looked into
the flames in the fireplace. He had laid aside his mask,
and now he rubbed his hands slowly together while
he considered word by word what he had overheard.

This Lady Jacinda—so she was to be thrust out of
sight, into a country Keep where her kin need not
look at her? Oh, he knew the old belief that a woman

carrying dared not see anything or anyone misshapen, lest it mark the babe in her womb. And Lord Vescys would certainly do all he could to assure the coming of a son. There would be no considering the Lady Jacinda. Did she care? Or would she be glad, as he had, to find a place away from sight of those who saw her not like them?

Had she longed to be free of that and would be pleased to come to Ghyll? And was it harder for her, a maid, to be so, than it was for him? For the first time Collard was pulled out of his dreams and his bitterness, to think of someone living, breathing, walking this world.

He arose and picked up the lamp. With it in hand, he went to a wall shelf and held the light to fully illumine the figures there. There were a goodly company of them, beasts and humanoid together. Looking upon them critically, something stirred in his mind, not quite a dream memory.

Collard picked several up, turned them about. Though he did not really look at them closely now, he was thinking. In the end he chose one which seemed right for his purpose.

Bringing the figure back to the table he laid out his tools. What he had was a small beast of horselike form. It was posed rearing, not as in battle but as if it gamboled in joyous freedom. But it was not a horse, for from between its delicate ears sprang a single horn.

Laying it on its side, Collard went to work on the base. It was cockcrow when he was done. And now the dancing unicorn had become a seal, its base graven to print a J with a small vine tracery about it.

Collard pushed back from the table. The need which had set him to work was gone. Why had he done this? He was tempted almost to sweep the piece into the melting pot so he could not see it again. But he did not, only pushed it away, determined to forget his folly.

He did not witness the entrance of the Lord Vescys and his daughter, though all the rest of Ghyll gathered. But he heard later that the Lady Jacinda came in a horse litter, and that she was so muffled by cloaks and covers that only her face could be seen. It was true that she was small and her face very pale and thin.

"Not make old bones, that one won't," he heard Nicala affirm. "I heard that Dame Matild has already sent for Sharvana. The lady brought only her old nurse and she is ailing, too. There will be no feasting at Ghyll Keep." There was regret in her voice, not, Collard believed, for the plight of the Lady Jacinda, but rather that the stir at the Keep would be soon over, with none of the coming and going which the villagers might enjoy as a change in their lives.

Collard ran fingers along the side of his mask. For all his care it was wearing thin. He might visit Sharvana soon. But why, his hard honesty made him face the truth, practice such excuses? He wanted to hear of the lady and how she did in a body which imprisoned her as his did him. So with the coming of dark he went. But at the last moment he took the seal, still two-minded over it.

There was a light in Sharvana's window. He gave his own private knock and slipped in at her call. To his surprise she sat on her stool by the fireplace, her journey cloak still about her shoulders, though its hood had slipped back. Her hands lay in her lap and there was a kind of fatigue about her he had never seen before.

Collard went to her quickly, took her limp hands in his.

"What is it?"

"That poor little one, Collard, cruel—cruel—"

"The Lady Jacinda?"

"Cruel," she repeated. "Yet she is so brave, speaking me fair and gentle even when I needs must hurt her poor body. Her nurse, ah, she is old and for all her love of her lady can do little to ease her. They traveled at a pace which must have wracked her. Yet I would judge she made no word of complaint. Just as she has never spoken out against her banishment, or so her nurse told me privately after I had given a

94

soothing draught and seen her asleep. But it is a cruel thing to bring her here—"

Collard squatted on his heels, listening. It was plain that the Lady Jacinda had won Sharvana's support. But at length she talked herself quiet and drank of the herb tea he brewed for her. Nor did she ask why he had come, seemed only grateful that he was there. At last, to shake her out of bleak thoughts, he took the seal out of his belt wallet and set it in the lamplight.

It had been fashioned of that same strange metal which had been his bane. He was drawing on that more and more, for it seemed to him that those pieces he fashioned of that were his best and came the closest to matching his dream memories. Now it glowed in the light.

Sharvana drew a deep breath, taking it up. When she looked upon the seal in the base she nodded.

"Well done, Collard. I shall see this gets to her hand—"

"Not so!" Now he wanted to snatch it back but somehow his hand would not obey his wish.

"Yes." She was firm. "And, Collard, if she asks—you will bring others. If for even the short space of the fall of a drop of water you can make her forget what her life is, then you have done a great thing. Bring to me the happy ones, those which will enchant her —perhaps even make her smile."

So Collard culled his collection, startled to find how few he had which were "happy." Thus he set to work, and oddly enough now his dream people he remembered as beautiful or with an amusing oddness.

Twice had he made visits to Sharvana with his offerings. He was working only with the strange metal now and found it easy to shape. But the third time she came to him, which was so unusual he was startled.

"The Lady Jacinda wants to see you, to thank you face to face."

"Face to face!" Collard interrupted her. His hands went up to cover even that mask in a double veiling of his "face."

Then Sharvana's eyes flashed anger. "You are—or you

95

were—no coward, Collard. Do you so fear a poor, sick maid who wants only to give you her thanks? She has fretted about this until it weighs on her mind. You have given her pleasure, do not spoil it. She knows how it is with you, and she has arranged for you to come by night, through the old posten gate, I with you. Do you now say 'no'?"

He wanted to, but found he could not. For there had grown in him the desire to see the Lady Jacinda. He had been, he thought, very subtle in his questioning of Sharvana, perhaps too subtle for the bits he had learned he had not been able to fit into any mind picture. Now he found himself agreeing.

Thus, with Sharvana as his guide, Collard came to the bower of the Lady Jacinda, trying to walk as straight as his crooked body would allow, his mask tightly fastened against all eyes, most of all hers.

She was very small, even as they said, propped with cushions and well covered with furred robes, as she sat in a chair which so overtopped her with its tall back that she seemed even smaller. Her hair was long and the color of dark honey, and it lay across her hunched shoulders in braids bound with bell-hung ribbons. But for the rest she was only a pale, thin face and two white hands resting on the edge of a board laid across her lap for a table. On that board marched all the people and beasts he had sent to her. Now and then she caressed one with a fingertip.

Afterward he could not really remember their greeting to one another. It was rather as if two old friends, long parted, came together after many seasons of unhappiness, to sit in the sun and just enjoy warmth and their encounter. She asked him of his work, and he told her of the dreams. And then she said something which did linger in his mind:

"You are blessed, Collard-of-the-magic-fingers, that you can make your dreams live. And I am blessed that you share them with me. Now—name these—"

Somehow he began to give names to each. And she nodded and said:

"That is just right! You have named it aright!"

It was a dream itself, he afterward thought, as he stumbled back to the village beside Sharvana, saying nothing as he wavered along, for he was reliving all he could remember, minute by minute.

With the morn he awoke after short hours of sleep with the urgency to be at work again. And he labored throughout the day with the feeling that this was a task which must be done and he had little time in which to do it.

What he wrought now was not any small figure but a hall in miniature—such a hall as would be found, not in the small Keep of Ghyll, but perhaps in the hold of a High Lord. Scented wood for paneling, metal —the strange metal wherever it could be used.

Exhausted, he slept. He ate at times when hunger pinched him hard, but time he did not count—nor how long before he had it done.

He sat studying it carefully, marking the furnishing. There were two high seats upon a dais. Those were empty—and that was not right. Collard rubbed his hand across his face, the rough scar tissue there for the first time meant nothing to him. There was something lacking—and he was so tired. He could not think.

He staggered away from the table, dropped upon his bed. And there he slept so deeply he believed he did not dream. Yet when he woke he knew what it was he must do. Again came that feeling of time's pressure, so he begrudged the moments it took to find food to eat.

Once more he wrought and worked with infinite care. When he had done, with that passing of time he did not mark, he had the two who must sit on those high seats and he placed them therein.

She—no twisted, humped body, but straight and beautiful, free to ride, to walk, to run as she never had been. Yet her face, it was Jacinda and none could deny it.

The man—Collard turned him around, surveying him carefully. No, this was no face he knew, but it had come to him as the right one. And when he put them both into the high hall, he looked about the hut with new eyes.

He rose and washed and dressed in his poor best, for to him for some years now clothing was merely to cover the body, not for pleasure. Then he put away all his tools, those he had made himself. Afterward he gathered up all the figures, those which were too grotesque or frightening, the first he had made. These he threw one by one into the melting pot.

Putting a wrapping of cloth about the hall he picked it up. It was heavy to carry and he must go slowly. But when he went outside the village was astir, lights of street torches such as were used only on great occasions were out. And the Keep was also strung with such torches.

A cold finger of fear touched Collard, and he hobbled by the back way to Sharvana's cottage. When he knocked upon her door he was sweating, though the wind of night was chill enough to bring shivers to those it nipped.

When she did not call, Collard was moved to do what he had never done before; his hand sought the latch and he entered unbidden. Strange scents filled the air and the light of two candles set one at either end of the table burned blue as he had never seen. Between those candles lay certain things he guessed were of the Wise Craft: a roll of parchment spread open with two strange-colored rocks to hold it so, a basin of liquid which shimmered and gave off small sparks, a knife crossed with a rune-carved wand.

Sharvana stood there, looking at him. He feared she might be angry at his coming, but it seemed more as if she had been waiting for him, for she beckoned him on. And though heretofore he had been shy of her secrets, this time he went to her, with the feeling that something was amiss and time grew shorter with each breath.

He did not set down his burden on the table until Sharvana, again without speaking, waved him to do so. She pulled free the cloth and in the blue candle flame the small hall—Collard gasped. For a moment or two it was as if he had stood at a distance and looked into room which was full-sized—real.

"So—that is the answer." Sharvana spoke slowly. She leaned closer, studying it all, as if she must make sure it was fit for some purpose of her own. She straightened again, her eyes now on Collard.

"Much has happened, you have not heard?"

"Heard what? I have been busied with this. The Lady Jacinda—?"

"Yes. The Lord Vescys died of a fever. It seems that his new lady was disappointed in those hopes which made it necessary to send the Lady Jacinda here. His only heir is his daughter. She is no longer forgotten, and by those who mean her no good. The Lady Gwennan has sent to fetch her—she is to be married forthwith to the Lady's brother Huthart, that they may keep the lands and riches. No true marriage, and how long may she live thereafter—with them wishing what she brings—not her?"

Collard's hands tightened on the edge of the table as he listened. Sharvana's words were a rain of blows, hurting more than any pain of body.

"She—she must not go!"

"No? Who is to stop her, to stand in the path of those who would fetch her? She has bought a little time by claiming illness, lying in bed. Her nurse and I together have afrighted the ladies of the household sent to fetch her by foreseeing death on the road. And that they fear—*before* she is wedded. Now they speak of the Lord Huthart riding here, wedding her on her deathbed if this be it."

"What—"

Sharvana swept on. "This night I called on powers which I have never dared to trouble before, as they can be summoned only once or twice by a Wise Woman. They have given me an answer—if you will aid—"

"How?"

"There is a shrine of the Old Ones—high in the northern craigs. That power which once dwelt there —perhaps it can be summoned again. But it must have a focus point to work through. You have that—" she

99

pointed to the hall. "There sits the Lady Jacinda as she should be, wrought of metal once worked by the Old Ones themselves. How better can power be summoned? But this must be taken to the shrine, and the time is very short."

Collard once more looped the cloth about the hall. He was sure of nothing now save that Sharvana herself believed in the truth of what she said. And if she was right— If she was wrong, what could he do? Try to strike down those who would take the lady away or wed her by force? He—the monster one?

Better believe that Sharvana was right. No one could deny that the Old Ones could still show power if they would; there were too many tales of such happenings. Sharvana had caught up a bag, pushed into it two unlit candles, a packet of herbs.

"Set what you carry on mid-stone," she told him, "light a candle on either side of it, even as you see them here. Give a pinch of herb powder to each flame when it is lit. Call then three times upon Talann. I shall go back to the Keep, do what I can to delay matters there. But hurry!"

"Yes." He was already on his way to the door.

Run he could not. The best he could produce was a shambling trot and that was hard to keep over rough ground. But at least he was near the craigs. Doubtless the house of the Wise Woman had always been there for a reason to be close to the shrine of the Old Ones.

Crossing the fields was not too hard, but the climb which followed taxed all his strength and wit. There was a path—perhaps in fairer weather was it easier to follow. But now it proved hard in the dark. Until Collard saw that there was a faint glow of light from what he carried, and he twitched off part of the cloth so that there was radiance from the metal showing.

Twice he slipped and fell, both times rising bruised and bloody, yet he kept on doggedly, more careful of what he carried than his own warped body. He was so tired that he must force himself on inch by painful inch. Now and again overlying that nightmare way he could see the white face of the Lady Jacinda, and there was that in her eyes which kept him struggling.

So he came to the ancient shrine. It was a cleft in the rock, smoothed by the arts of men—or whatever creatures once gathered here—and there was a band of badly eroded carving. Collard thought he could make out in that hints of his dream creatures. But he focused his attention to the stone set directly before the cleft. It was shaped like the crescent moon, its horns pointing outward so Collard stood between them as he set the hall on the altar and took away the covering.

With shaking hands he put up the candles, drew out his tinderbox to light them. Then the pinch of herb for each. His hand shook so he had to steady it with the other as he followed Sharvana's orders.

There was a puff of scented smoke. Collard leaned against the moon altar as he cried out in the best voice he could summon—no louder than the hoarse croak of a fen frog:

"Talann, Talann, Talann!"

Collard did not know what he expected. The Old Power was fearsome—he might be blasted where he stood. But when nothing came, he fell to the ground, not only overcome by weariness, but in black despair of mind. Old Power—perhaps too old and long since gone!

Then—was it in his mind?—or did it echo from the rocks about him, tolled in some deep voice as if the ridge itself gave tongue?

"What would you?"

Collard did not try to answer in words; he was too dazed, too awed. He made of his feelings a plea for the Lady Jacinda.

From where he crouched on the frost-chilled rock his eyes were on a level with the hall. It shone in splendor, more and more as if a hundred, a thousand lamps were lit within. He thought he could hear a distant murmur of voices, a sound of lute-playing—warmth—sweet odors—and life—swelling life!

For Jacinda—life for her! Like this—as it should have been! No words—just the knowledge that this was what

101

should have been had matters not gone fearfully astray in another time and place.

Warmth—light—around him! He was not crouched in the cold, he was sitting—looking down a hall—around him— No! For a moment he remembered what must be the truth—he was dreaming again!

But this dream—he pushed aside all doubts. This dream he could claim, it was his to keep, to hold forever! His dream—and hers!

Collard turned his head. She was watching him, a small smile on her lips, welcoming— And in her eyes —what glory in her eyes! He put forth his hand and hers came quickly to meet it.

"My lord—"

For a moment he was troubled. "We dream—"

"Do we? Then let us claim this dream together, and claiming it, make it real!"

He did not quite understand, but she answered his uncertainty somehow. He began to forget, as she had already resolutely forgotten.

There was a shining pool of strange metal on the altar. It began to flow, to cascade to the ground, to sink into the waiting earth which would safe-hide it forever.

In the Keep Sharvana and the nurse each snuffed a candle by a curtained bed, nodded thankfully to one another.

But in the hall wrought by Collard there was high-feasting and an everlasting dream.

# AMBER OUT OF QUAYTH

# 1

Bees DRONED in the small walled garden, working to store their harvest before the coming of the Ice Dragon. Ysmay sat back on her heels, pushed a wandering tendril of hair from her eyes with an earth-streaked hand. Her own harvest lay spread behind her on a well-cured hide. Those herbs would be dried in the hut at the other end of the garden.

But when she stooped to cut and pull there was no answering clink from her girdle. She was not yet used to that loss. Sometimes she would find herself feeling for the keys she no longer wore, afraid (until she remembered) that she might have lost them during her digging and delving, pulling and cutting.

She had lost them indeed, those weighty responsibilities of the Uppsdale chatelaine, but not because they had left her belt by chance. No, they swung elsewhere now, Annet was lady in this hold. As if it were possible to forget that ever—though here in this one small place Ysmay could still claim sovereignty.

For five years, she had worn those keys. They had been at first frightening years, during which she had to learn much that was more demanding than the lore of herbs. Then the years had brought pride. She, a woman, so ordered life within the Dale that people lived with a measure of content, though the sharp edge of hunger's sword, the shadow of fear's mace, were ever over them.

In the end news came that the war in High Hallack was done, the invaders driven into the sea, or hunted like winter wolves to their snarling deaths. Men returned to their homes—some men. Among them not her father, nor her brother Ewald—they were long lost. But Gyrerd had ridden home with a ragged tail of the hold's menie. And with him Annet, who was daughter to Urian of Langsdale, now his bride and lady. Ysmay's tongue swept across her upper lip to taste the salt of her own sweat. But that was not as bitter as the salt of her life with Annet.

Now Ysmay truly lived under ill-faced stars. From ruler in the hold she had become a nithling, less than one of the kitchen wenches—for such had their duties, she none, save what lay within this garden—and that only because for Annet seedlings would not grow. Though Annet resented this with a bitterness she showed to Ysmay when she had opportunity, those with ills to be cured still came to their lord's sister, not to his lady wife. For Ysmay had the healing hands.

Healing hands, yet she could not heal the ache in her heart, her emptiness. Pride she still had, and that stubbornness which faced defeat shield up, sword ready. Bleak indeed might the future stretch before her, but it would be a future of her own devising. At that thought a shadow smile curved her lips. Ha, Annet had thought to send her to the Ladies of the Shrine. But the Abbess Grathulda was a match for the Lady Annet. She knew well that Ysmay was not of the stuff of a Shrine Daughter. Passive she might school herself to be, but there was an inner fire in her which could not be quenched in prayers and ritual.

Sometimes that fire blazed high in her. But not even her own waiting wench knew the night hours when Ysmay paced her cramped chamber, thinking or trying to think of some way out of the trap.

Had these been normal times, had her father survived, she might have followed custom, gone to rule by marriage another hold. It could be that she would not even see her lord before their marriage day, but that was proper. As a wife she would have certain rights which none could gainsay her, those same rights which Annet held here.

But she had no father to arrange such a match. And, what was worse, no dowry to attract a suitor. War had cut too deeply the resources of the dale. Gyerd, being what he was, would not lessen what he had left. His sister could go to the Ladies, or remain on grudging sufferance, which Annet could make as cold as winter.

The rebellion so hot in Ysmay was gaining strength. She willed it under her control, breathing deeply of the strongly scented air, making her mind consider what lay directly before her. She examined the plants she chose with deliberate care, when she wanted to tear and destroy in her frustration.

"Ysmay—sister!" Annet's sweetly reasonable voice was a lash across her shoulders.

"I am here," she answered tonelessly.

"News—most welcome news, sister!"

What, Ysmay wondered. She edged around, her dun-colored skirts kilted in a sprawl about long limbs which Annet's daintiness made seem so clumsy and out of proportion.

The Lady of Uppsdale stood just within the gate. Her skirts were the deep blue of the autumn sky. At her neck the silver beads winked in the light. Her hair, braided and looped high, was almost as silvery. In all she gave the impression of comeliness, if one did not note the thinness of those ever-smiling lips, or see that the smile was absent from her eyes.

"News?" Ysmay's voice was harsh in her own ears. It was ever so. She need only sense Annet near and she became what the other thought her—as if those thoughts produced some shape-changing magic—clumsy, loutish.

"Yes—a fair, sister! Such a fair as they had in the old days! A rider from Fyndale brings the news."

Ysmay caught some of Annet's enthusiasm. A fair! Dimly she could remember the last fair in Fyndale. Through the mist of years, that memory had taken on a golden glory. Her reason told her that was not so, but her memory continued to trick her.

"A fair, and we shall go!" Annet made one of those pretty and appealing gestures which so enchanted any male in sight, clapping her hands together as might a little maid.

We? Did Annet mean Ysmay too? She doubted that. But the other was continuing.

"My lord says that it is safe now, that he need only

106

leave a token force here. Ysmay—is this not fair fortune? Hasten, sister, you must come and look through the chests with me. Let us see what we can find that we shame not our lord."

I know what I can find in any chest of mine, Ysmay thought without pleasure. But it would seem that she was indeed to be included in their party. And she knew a swift rush of excitement which was akin to pleasure as she gathered up her morning's harvest.

Though she knew Annet was no friend to her, Ysmay could not fault her during the following days. Annet had a clever eye for dress and, from the few pieces of old finery of her own mother's time which Ysmay possessed, she pieced out two robes of more subtle cut than any Ysmay had ever owned. When she faced the burnished shield which served as her mirror, on the morning of their going, she thought she looked well indeed.

Never had Ysmay any pretense of the soft prettiness of Annet. Her face narrowed from cheekbones to a pointed chin, her mouth was far too large for her face. Her nose—there was no denying it was too high in the bridge. Her eyes were merely eyes, their color seemed to vary, being now green, again darkly brown. Her hair was thick enough, but it was not golden, nor richly black, just brown. Her skin, not properly pale, was also brown from her labors in the garden, the more so this season when she had been driven to spend more and more time there.

She was too tall for a woman, she had always known that. But in this robe—well, she looked more as a woman should look. It was made of an odd shade of tawny, just like—Ysmay turned to the small box which had been her mother's and took out a small amulet. Yes, it was the hue of this robe, was her amber talisman. The small piece she held was old and so worn she could barely distinguish the carving, but it was a warm, beautiful color. She found a cord to string it on and knotted it as a pendant.

For safekeeping she tucked it within the neck of the laced bodice. Her dress was made with divided

skirt for riding, but to Ysmay it held all the enchant-
ment of a court gown.

Though she was wary, she found little to worry her
as she rode with Annet. Gyrerd was ahead with his
marshal, the body of the household straggling behind.
Those who had mounts rode them at an ambling pace,
others walked, for the promise of the fair gave good
cheer above aching feet.

They left Uppsdale at dawn. At nooning they were
at the south gate of the dale where they feasted on
cold food. That night they reached the outer rim of
Fyndale itself and camped in company with another
party, the Lord of Marchpoint, his lady, daughter and
their following. There was much coming and going
with exchange of news and rumors.

Ysmay listened, but talked little. One thing she heard
gave her a thought to dwell upon. The Lady Dairine,
daughter of Marchpoint, coyly confessed her hopes to
Ysmay. One of the great advantages which might be
found at the fair was a future husband.

"My lady mother," Dairine offered as final evidence,
"in the days before the war, of course, went to the
fair at Ulmsport—which was a far greater gathering than
this, sought by the highest of the Lords. It was there
my father first saw her. And before he rode thence
he had talk with her father. The matter was so settled
that their betrothal was held at Midwinter Feast."

"I wish you the same luck," Ysmay answered, her
thoughts busy. Was this why Annet and Gyrerd had
brought her? But without a dowry what match could
she attract?

A proper match? With half the lords and their heirs
dead in the war, there could well be many maids never
wifed. So—what then of those who had been shieldless men, newcomers without family names for kin
blood? They had heard tales of masterless men who
would now be master, men who had taken over abandoned holdings, calling themselves lord, with none to
challenge them.

But such would be shrewd enough to drive hard
bargains when it came to taking a wife. They might

want kinship with old names, but they would also want a dowry. Would all do so? Ysmay felt a stir of a new excitement. What if—what if the most unexpected could happen?

She thought of Uppsdale which had been her world. It was not her world any longer, it was Annet's. She believed now and was sure this was true, that she could turn her back on Uppsdale if the future offered her a place of her own.

The fair was where it had been before, in the view of the gray stone pillar. The pillar remained from earlier days, when the men of High Hallack had not yet come to Fyndale. An older people had vanished before the coming of the Dalesmen.

Their traces held power of a sort—which troubled the Dalesmen. To pry too deeply might unleash that which could not easily be controlled. So there was awe and respect for old monuments. And at Fyndale all who were the heads of households went directly to the pillar, laying their bared hands upon it and swearing peace, so that no feuds or old rivalries could disturb the fair.

Fronting the pillar the booths of the merchants were set up in a wide curve. At a little distance, on fields yellow with the stubble of cut grain, sprouted the tents and flimsy leantos of the visitors. There the party from Uppsdale rode to set up temporary lodging.

"Ten merchants' flags, sister." Annet, flushed of face, bright of eye, slapped her gloves into the palm of one hand. "Ten merchants of consequence, perhaps even some from Ulmsport! Think of it!"

It had indeed been a long time since merchants of such standing had come into the upper Dales. Ysmay was as eager as the rest to see what lay in those booths. Not that she had aught to spend. But even to look would be a feast for the eyes, something to remember during drab future days. They had hardly expected to find merchants of the flag class.

Annet, Ysmay, and the two ladies of Marchpoint went to explore the booths. What the traders had to offer might be poor after the long years of war and the failure of overseas trade, but it was still far more than they had.

The Lady of Marchpoint had a round of silver to lay out in the booth of woven stuffs. It was to be spent, Lady Dairine proudly told Ysmay in a whisper, for a length to make at least an over-tunic, to be kept for her wedding. And the spending of such a sum took caution and bargaining.

They studied several lengths of heavy silk. None was new, some even had small needle holes unpicked from earlier sewing. Loot, Ysmay suspected, perhaps found among the pickings when the invaders' camps were overrun. She loved the rich coloring, but thought she would not care to wear anything made of plunder. Thought of the previous owner would have troubled her.

There were laces too. They also had the appearance of former use. But the merchant had some bolts of less rich stuffs. These were well dyed (Ysmay was sure she recognized the colors from her own experiments) warm and excellently woven. Those she coveted more than the lengths the Lady of Marchpoint fussed over.

It was hot in the booth, even though the front was looped up. At last she moved to the opening, looking away from the temptation of those fabrics she could not buy.

So Ysmay witnessed the arrival of Hylle, an impressive sight, for he led in a train of men and pack-beasts to rival that of a Dale lord. He had no flag at the van to label him merchant, nor did he come close to the booths already set up, but rather waved his following to a site at one side, keeping aloof from the company of his kind.

His men were shorter than most Dalesmen and, in the unusual bulk of clothing they had upon them, looked squat, clumsy, though they worked with speed and assurance, setting up booth poles, unrolling walls and roof of hides to be stretched over the frame. In spite of the heat, the workers wore their head hoods

110

pulled well down, so Ysmay could not see their faces, a fact which made her uneasy.

However the master was in full view. He had not dismounted and his mount was a good one, fully equal to any a Dale lord would be proud to bestride. He sat with one hand on his hip, the other playing with the reins, watching the efforts of his followers.

Even in the saddle he loomed tall, and looked more warrior than merchant—though in these days a man must be both if he would protect his goods. He wore no sword, but there was a long knife at his belt. Fastened to his saddle was a light battle mace.

Unlike his followers he had bared his head, his riding cap hanging from his saddle horn. His hair was very dark and his face curiously pale for a man out in all weathers on the roads. He was not handsome by Dale standards, yet once you had looked upon him, you could not easily turn your eyes away. Rather you found yourself scanning him intently as if you could so read what manner of man he was.

He had sharp features, a mouth set straight as if used little to expressing emotion, black brows across his nose to form a single bar. The color of his eyes Ysmay could not see, for his lids drooped as if he were sleepy. Yet she did not doubt that he saw all about him, and had thoughts concerning what he saw.

There was that which hinted that he wore an outer self which was not the same as his spirit. Ysmay decided her fancies must be more controlled—still the impression clung that here was a man few would ever know. She believed he would be worth knowing nonetheless. She felt heat rising in her cheeks, and inner disturbance she had not known before.

Ysmay turned sharply away, aware her stare had been too intent. She hurried back to the others and stood gazing at the length of rose silk the Lady of Marchpoint had chosen, not seeing a thread of it.

They did not visit Hylle's booth, since he had not opened for business. It was not until they ate their evening meal that Ysmay learned what wares he had brought to the fair and that his name was Hylle.

"From the north," Gyrerd said. "Amber—they say a real treasure in amber. But he has chosen ill. I do not believe there is enough coin here to buy more than two beads of it! His name is Hylle, but his men are a queer crew—keeping to themselves, not even sending for a jug of Mamer's autumn ale."

Amber! Ysmay's hand sought the amulet beneath her bodice. Yes, this merchant Hylle would find few here to buy such. But like enough he was on his way to Ulmsport and had only stopped along the road, hearing of the fair. Amber—she knew where her own piece had come from—the cleft of a hill-born stream. Once there had been more. Fifty years ago, amber had brought riches to Uppsdale. But that was before a fall of rock had sealed the source.

She smiled ruefully. Were that not so, why, she would be the one to wear not only amber, but gold. She would not have to haggle for a length of old, needle-pricked silk from some looter's spoil—but that barren hillside which now hid the amber for all time had been sealed even to Ysmay's mother. And on her mother's dying it had come to her. Nothing was there now but stone and a few stunted trees, and most had forgotten that a piece of ground, without price or use, was hers.

"Amber—" Annet repeated, her eyes shining as they had when she had earlier looked upon the silks. "My lord, amber is a powerful thing, it can cure. The Ladies of Grayford had a necklet of amber and those who were taken with evils in the throat wore it with a blessing so it wrought their cure. Yet it is beautiful also, like honey grown hard, so its sweetness abides. Let us go and look upon this Hylle's wares!"

Gyrerd laughed. "My dear lady, such sweetness is beyond the purse at my belt. I might well pledge the whole of Uppsdale and not raise enough to buy such a necklet as you spoke of."

Ysmay's hand tightened. For, while the amulet was hers, if Annet saw it, could Ysmay continue to keep it? Annet had taken all else, but this was not for her grasping hands.

"He will find few buyers here," Annet said thought-fully. "But if he sets up a booth, he must show what he has. And maybe—with so few buyers—"

"You think he will ask less? Perhaps you are right, my lady. Only do not make big eyes and sigh, for there is no hope. Not because I would say you nay for a whim, but because I have no choice."

Though the dark of twilight was already here they went to where Hylle's booth was marked by blazing torches, tended by two of his men, still keeping their hoods, their faces shadowed.

As they passed one man, Ysmay tried to see him better, but could not distinguish his features. She felt only a shrinking as one might from something mis-shapen, not by the whim of nature, but because of in-ner blight. Again she chid herself for being fanciful and hurried after the others.

# 2

RICH COLOR was here, not in draped lengths of material, but laid out on tables. Here was worked am-ber in such quantity as Ysmay would not have be-lieved existed.

Nor was it all the honey amber. It ranged through subtle shades, each laid on a backing to enhance it —pale, near to white, bright yellow of butter, red-dish, bluish, greenish. And it was wrought into neck-laces, armlets, bow-guards, girdles, set into the hilts of swords and knives, in rings, in circlets for the head. There were larger pieces which were bowls or gob-lets, or small figures of gods and demons—

Facing that display the party from Uppsdale came to a halt, staring as fieldworkers might do if suddenly transported to the feast hall of a lord.

"Welcome, Lord, Ladies." Hylle bowed, not in the obeisant greeting of a merchant, but as though he dealt equal to equal. He clapped his hands and two of his hooded men shambled out to put stools to the middle table. Another brought a tray of cups with a greeting drink.

Ysmay saw the uncertainty of her brother. He was jealous of his rank, claimed due reverence from a shieldless man. Still he accepted a cup, drank to Hylle, and the women did likewise.

The drink was spicy rather than sweet and Ysmay held it in her mouth, trying to guess the mixture of herbs in its making. But with all her learning she could not be sure. Still holding the cup she sat content to look about.

There must be more than a High Lord's hold ransom in value here and she wondered at the folly— or courage—of a man venturing overland with this in such unsettled times. Folly? She looked at Hylle. No folly in his face, only courage and something else, an assurance close to arrogance.

"Riches, Merchant." She had missed the first of Gyrerd's speech. "Too rich for us here. We have felt the hard hand of the invader too heavily to make good customers."

"War is harsh." Hylle's voice was low but deep. "It spares no man, even the victors. And in the time of war, trade is deeply wounded. It has been many years since Quayth's amber has been shown in any market place. So to water trade that it may sprout and grow, prices are lower—even for such as this—" He caught up a necklace of many pendants.

Ysmay heard a sigh from Annet. Her own hunger awoke also. Yet—there was something— She pressed her hand once again on Gunnora's charm and, as she did so, she felt sudden distaste for what she saw, perhaps because there was so much of it. Heaped so together its beauty seemed belittled, diminished.

"Quayth?" Gyrerd made of that name a question.

"To the north, my lord. As you know amber is found on the shore of the sea in certain places, or along streams. The ignorant say it is the casting of dragons, but that is not so. Rather is it a hardened gum exuded from trees thousands of seasons dead. In Quayth there must once have been a mighty forest of such trees,

for amber is easily found—easily I say in comparison
to other places.

"Also you see here the fruit of many years of collection when because of the war it could not be offered generally for sale. So that this is more than would
be in one place in the natural order of things."

He replaced the necklace and picked up a broad
pendant wrought into a shape Ysmay could not clearly
see.

"Now here you have a talisman of Thunder Shield,
an older piece. See you the difference?" He held it
closer to an armlet. "The older it is, the longer exposed to the air and handling, the more amber takes
on a deeper and richer coloring."

He put back the armlet but continued to hold the
pendant. There was a slight change in his expression.
It seemed to Ysmay that he was looking with a searching intensity at Gyrerd, and then to Annet. Finally
those dark eyes, whose color she could not name, were
turned in her direction, as if to draw from her, even
against her will an answer to some unknown question.

"Quayth seems to be well favored," Gyrerd said. "Better by far than Uppsdale in our grandfather's time."

Hylle's eyes swung from Ysmay. She had been un-
comfortable, wondering what there was about her to
catch and hold his attention.

"Uppsdale, my lord?" Hylle's tone invited an explanation.

"There was a rock cut which yielded some amber,
enough to make life smoother," Gyrerd replied. "But
later a fall of rock, such a slide as no man could dig
through, sealed it. If any remains there it is useless as
if it lay at the bottom of the sea."

"A sad loss, my lord," nodded Hylle.

Annet rose from her stool, wandered from table
to table. Now and then she put forth a finger to touch
a necklace, a skillfully wrought circlet of amber flowers and leaves for the hair. But Ysmay stayed where
she was, watching Hylle from beneath lowered lids.
She knew that he was as aware of her as she of him.

There was a heady excitement in this centering upon a man. Yet he was only a merchant.

At last they left and, when they were out of the booth, Ysmay drew a deep breath. One of the hooded servants was detaching a burned torch from its standard to replace it. His hands were covered with gloves which was strange, for those were only worn by commoners in the coldest weather. But strangest of all was the fact that each finger and thumb tip was provided with a hooked claw extending for a noticeable distance, as if to resemble those of a beast of prey. Ysmay could not conceive of any reason to so embellish a hand covering. Dalesmen had many superstitions. Protective amulets were common, was there not one such about her neck? Suppose these strangers wore as protective magic the claws of some animal? With this answer her mind was more at ease.

But she could not forget how Hylle had stared at her. She discovered that her answering excitement lingered. So that she held his face in mind and tried also to picture the Quayth from which he had come and what his life must be there.

Vaguely she heard Annet prattle of the necklace. And then came a single sentence which awoke her abruptly from her dream.

"But my lord, remains there nothing then of the amber found at Uppsdale? Surely your grandfather did not barter it all!"

"It went during the lean years, sweetling. I remember that my mother had an amulet left once—"

Ysmay's hand was to her breast in protection. Annet had taken all else, and that she had had to yield. But Gunnora's charm was hers! And she would fight for it.

"But is it true that the place where it came from could not be reopened—" Annet persisted.

"Too true. My father, when it was sure war would come, needed treasure for weapons. He brought in a man used to the iron mines of the South Ridges, paying well for his opinion. But the fellow swore no skill could shift that rock fall."

Ysmay felt small relief. At least Annet did not ask

more about remaining amber. She excused herself and
went to her pallet.

But not to sleep easily. When she did it was with
her hand closed protectively about Gunnora's amulet.
She dreamed, but when she awoke she could not remember those dreams, though she carried into waking the feeling they had been important.

The Lady of Marchpoint and Dairine came in the
morning, excited over Hylle's wares. Again they had
hard money to lay out. And seeing Annet's mouth droop,
Gyrerd hacked one of the silver rings from his sword
belt.

"If he lays his prices low to gain a market," he said,
"get you a-fairing. More than this I cannot do."

Annet said her thanks quickly. Experience had taught
her how far her demands might go.

So, somewhat against her will, Ysmay returned to
Hylle's booth. This time his hooded servants were not
visible. But within the door, on a stool, squatted a
woman of strange aspect.

She was thick of body, her round head seeming to
rest directly on her shoulders, as if she possessed no
neck. Like the hooded men, she was dressed in a robe
of drab hue but hers was patterned over with symbols in thick black-and-white yarn.

Her girdle was of the same black and white mingled together. Now her fat hands rested on her knees,
palms up as if she waited for alms, and she stared into
them. She might have been holding a scroll from which
she read.

Strings of coarse yellow hair hung from under a veil
fastened with braiding. Her face was broad, with a straggling of hairs on the upper lip and along the paunchy
jaw.

If she had been left as guardian of the booth, she
was a poor one, for she did not look up as the ladies
approached, but continued to stare absorbedly at her
empty hands. Only when Ysmay passed her, did she
raise her eyes.

"Fortunes, fair ladies." Her voice was in contrast to
her lumpish, toadlike body, being soft and singsong.

"A reading of pins on the Stone of Esinore, or, if you fancy, the foretelling of what the Elder Gods have written on your hands."

Annet shook her head impatiently. At another time she might have been tempted. Now she had silver and a chance to spend it to the best of her bargaining powers. Nor was Ysmay ready to listen. That there were true seeresses, no one doubted. But she did not think this repulsive hag was one.

"Trust that which you wear, Lady—" For the first time the woman looked directly at her. The soft voice was very low, plainly meant for her alone.

And Ysmay found herself, against her will, listening. Hylle came out of the shadows.

"Ninque seems to have a message for you, Lady. She is a true seeress, esteemed in Quayth."

This was not Quayth, Ysmay thought. Seeress or no, I do not want to listen to her. Yet she sat on the stool Hylle produced, to find herself eye to eye with the woman.

"Your hand upon mine, Lady, so that I may read what lies there."

Ysmay's hand half moved to obey. Then she jerked back, her disgust for the woman overriding whatever spell the other cast. The woman showed no emotion, only her eyes continued to hold Ysmay's.

"You have more than you believe, Lady. You are one for far faring and deeds beyond the women's bowers. You—no, I cannot read clearly. There is that under your touch now—bring it forth!"

Her soft, insinuating voice was a bark of order. Before she thought Ysmay pulled at the cord, drawing out Gunnora's amulet. And behind her she heard a hiss of indrawn breath.

"Amber." Again the seeress' voice was singsong. "Amber in your hand always, Lady. It is your fate and your fortune. Follow where it leads and you shall have your heart's full desire."

Ysmay stood up. She jerked from her belt purse a single copper coin and dropped it into those hands, forcing herself to give the conventional thanks for fore-seeing, though the words choked her.

"A good fortune, Lady," Hylle stepped between her and the woman. "That bit you wear—it is very old—"

She sensed he would like to examine it, but she had no intention of letting it out of her hands.

"It is Gunnora's talisman. I had it from my mother."

"A sign of power for any woman." He nodded. "Odd-ly enough I do not have its like here. But let me show you a thing which is very rare—" He put two fingers to her hanging sleeve. And it was as if the world sud-denly narrowed to the two of them alone.

He picked up a box of fragrant pinsal wood, slid off its lid. Within was a cylinder of amber, a small pillar of golden light. Caught within it for the cen-turies was a winged creature of rainbow beauty.

Ysmay had seen in her own amulet small seeds, which was meet for a talisman of Gunnora's, the har-vest goddess of fertile fields and fertile woman. But this piece was marked with no random pattern of seeds. It was as if the creature had been fixed by intelligent purpose.

So beautiful it was that she gasped. Hylle put it into the hands she had involuntarily stretched forth and she turned it around and around, studying it from all angles. Ysmay could not be sure whether the creature within was a small bird or a large insect, for it was new to her, perhaps something which had long gone from the living world.

"What is it?"

Hylle shook his head. "Who knows? Yet once it lived. One finds such in amber from time to time. Still this is unusual."

"Sister—what have you?" Annet crowded in. "Ah, that is indeed a thing to look upon! Yet—one cannot wear it—"

Hylle smiled. "Just so. It is a wall ornament only."

"Take it," Ysmay held it out. "It is too precious to finger lightly." At that moment she coveted the flying thing greatly.

"Precious, yes. But there are other things. Lady, would you trade your amulet for this?"

He had stood the cylinder on the flattened palm of his hand, balanced it before her eyes to tempt her. But the moment of weakness was gone.

"No," she replied evenly.

Hylle nodded. "And you are very right, Lady. There is a virtue in such amulets as yours."

"What amulet, sister?" Annet crowded closer. "Where got you any amulet of price?"

"Gunnora's charm which was my mother's." Reluctantly Ysmay opened her hand to show it.

"Amber! And Gunnora's! But you are no wedded wife with a right to Gunnora's protection!" Annet's pretty face showed for an instant what really lay behind it. She was no whole friend, nor half friend, but really revealed herself as—unfriend.

"It was my mother's and is mine." Ysmay pushed the charm back under the edge of her bodice. Then she spoke to Hylle.

"For your courtesy in showing me this treasure, Master Trader, I give thanks."

He bowed as if she were the favorite daughter of a High Lord. But she was already turning out of the booth, uncertain of where to go or what to do. She was sure that Annet would now work upon Gyrerd to take her only treasure from her.

Yet Annet, upon her return to their tent, said nothing of the amulet. Rather she was displaying with open joy a bracelet of butter amber, its bright yellow contrasting with clasp and hinge of bronze. That she had purchased it with her single piece of silver she took as a tribute to her bargaining skill. And Ysmay hoped she was now fully satisfied.

However, she steeled herself to be on guard when they met for their evening meal. Gyrerd admired the bracelet and Ysmay waited tensely for Annet to introduce the subject of the amulet. Instead it was her brother who at last brushed aside the continued exclamations of his wife and turned to Ysmay, eyeing her as if moved by curiosity.

"We may have had more than one stroke of luck from Hylle's booth," he began.

"The amber mine!" Annet broke in. "My dear lord, does he know of a way that it can be worked again?"

"He thinks so."

"Ah, lucky, lucky day! Lucky chance that brought us to this fair!"

"Perhaps lucky, perhaps not so." He kept a sober face. "The mine, if it still holds aught, is not sealed to the Hold."

Annet's face grew sharp. "How so?" she demanded.

"It was settled upon Ysmay for a marriage portion."

"What fool—" Annet shrilled.

For the first time Gyrerd turned a frowning face upon her. "It was sealed to my mother. There were still hopes then that it might be worked and my father wished her secure against want. The dowry she brought rebuilt the north tower for the protection of the Dale. When she died, it was sealed to Ysmay."

"But the Dale is war-poor, it is now needed for the good of all!"

"True. But there is a way all may be satisfied. I have had talk with this Hylle. He is no common merchant, not only because of his wealth, but because he is lord in Quayth, of blood not unequal to our own. For some reason he has taken a fancy to Ysmay. If we betroth her to him, he will return half the amount of any amber he takes from the mine, using his own methods to open it again. See, girl?" He nodded to Ysmay. "You will get you a lord with greater riches than most hereabouts can claim, a hold where you carry the keys, and a full life for a woman. This is such a chance as you shall not find twice."

She knew that was true. And yet—what did she know of Hylle, save that he held her thoughts as no other man had done? What did she know of his northern hold? Where would he lead if she gave her consent? On the other side of the shield was the knowledge that, if she refused, Annet would surely make life a torment, nor would Gyrerd be pleased with her.

Looking from right to left, then right again, she thought she had little choice.

Quayth could not offer her worse than Uppsdale, were she to say yes. And there was hope it would offer better. After all, most marriages in the Dales were made so, between strangers. Few girls knew the men they went to bed with on their marriage night.

"I shall agree, if matters are as he has told you," she said slowly.

"Dear sister." Annet beamed on her. "What joy! You shall have better faring than this dame of Marchpoint buys to dress her cow-faced daughter! And such a wedding feast as all the Dales shall remember! My lord," she said to Gyrerd, "give you free-handed that your sister may go to her bridal as becomes one of high name."

"First we shall have the betrothal," he said, but in his voice also was an eager note. "Ah, sister, perhaps you have brought the best of fortune to Uppsdale!"

But Ysmay wondered. Perhaps she had been too quick to give her word. And now there was no drawing back.

# 3

ALL THE LAMPS in the great hall were alight, for it was close to winter and shadows were thick. But Gyrerd did not scant on his sister's wedding feast, as not only the lamps but the food on the table testified.

Ysmay was glad that custom decreed the bride keep her eyes on the plate she shared with the groom. He was courteous in asking her taste in dishes, waiting for her first choice, but she ate only a token bite or two.

She had assented to betrothal; today she gave her word in marriage. Now she wanted only escape, from the hall, from this man. What folly was hers? Was she so mean-spirited that she must give all she had for freedom from Annet's petty spite? As for Gyrerd, he

was so intent upon opening the old mine that *his* reaction to a refusal would not have been petty.

This was the natural way of life. A woman married
to benefit her House, her kin. If happiness followed,
then she was blessed indeed. Ysmay could hope for
that, but not expect it in the natural order of things.
And certainly he whom she had wedded would give
her rule over hearth and hold.

Hylle had ridden in for the wedding with but a
small train of followers and men-at-arms, but not the
hooded laborers. They were newly hired for protection he said, since his own people were not weapon-
trained. On the morrow, before the breath of the Ice
Dragon frosted the ground into iron, his workers would
try to reopen what rocks had closed.

Though Hylle had more than picks and spades. At
Gyrerd's persistent questioning, he had admitted to a
discovery of his own, a secret which he would not
explain, but which he believed would serve.

Ysmay had not looked straightly at him since their
hands had been joined before the niche of the house
spirit. He made a brave showing, she knew, his tunic
of a shade close to golden amber, with wrist bands,
collar and belt of that gem. His bride gifts rested heavily on her—girdle, necklace, a circlet on her unbound
hair—all of various shades of amber set together to
simulate flowers and leaves.

The feast had been long, but they were close to the
end. And if she had her will she would turn back
time to live these past hours over—so the moment
would not come when he would rise and take her
hand while those in the hall drank good fortune, and
those at the high table took up lamps to escort them to
the guest chamber.

Her heart beat in pounding leaps, her mouth was
dry, yet the palms of her hands were wet until she
longed to wipe them upon her skirt. Pride kept her
from that betraying gesture. Pride must be her support now, and she held to it.

The signal was given, the company arose. For a second of panic Ysmay thought her trembling legs would

not support her, that she would not have strength to walk the hall, climb the stairs. But somehow she did it. And she did not lean upon his arm. He must not guess, no one must guess her fear!

She clung to that as they stood at the foot of the great curtained bed. The scent of sweet herbs, crushed underfoot in a fresh laid carpet, fought with the smell of lamp oil, the odor of wine and of heated bodies, making her faintly ill. She was so intent upon holding to her mask of composure that she did not hear the bawdy jests of the company.

Had Hylle been one of their own they might have lingered. But there was that about him which fostered awe. So they tried none of the tricks common at such times. When they were gone, leaving but two great candles, one on either side of the chest at the foot of the bed, he crossed the room and set the lock-bar at the door.

"My lady." He returned to the chest whereon was a pitcher of wine, a platter of honey cakes. "I must share with you a secret of import."

Ysmay blinked. He was not the eager bridegroom, but rather spoke with the same tone as when he talked with Gyrerd about the mine. His attitude steadied her.

"I have spoken of my secret to open the mine. But I did not say how I came by it. I am a merchant, yes, and I hold the lordship of Quayth, make no mistake in that!" For a moment it was as if he faced a challenge. "But I have other interests. I am an astrologer and an alchemist, a seeker of knowledge along strange paths. I read the star messages as well as those of the earth.

"Because I do this I must sacrifice certain ways of mankind for a space. If I would succeed in what I do here, I cannot play husband to any woman. For all my strength is needed elsewhere. Do you understand?"

Ysmay nodded. But a new fear stirred. She had heard of the disciplines of the magics.

"Well enough." He was brisk now. "I had thought you were one of sensible mind, able to accept matters as they are. We shall, I am certain, deal well together. Let only this be understood between us from this hour forward. There are things in my life which are mine alone, not to be watched or questioned. I shall have a part of Quayth into which you venture not. I shall go on journeys of which you shall ask nothing, before or after.

"In return you shall have rulership of my household. I think you will find this to your liking. As for now, get you to bed. This night I must study the stars that I find the rightful time to turn my power against the stubborn rocks guarding your dowry."

Ysmay lay back on the pillows of the bed, around which Hylle himself had pulled the curtains, cutting off her sight of him. She could hear him move about the chamber, with now and then the clink of metal against metal, or against stone. For now she felt only relief, not curiosity.

She thought she could accept the life he outlined with a right good will. Let him have his secrets, and she her household. She thought of her chest of herb seeds and roots, ready corded to take to Quayth. Alchemist he had said—well, she, too, had her knowledge of distilling and brewing. If Quayth had not such a garden as she had tended here, it would gain one. Fitting one plan to another, she fell asleep, unmindful of what went on beyond the closed curtain.

It was noon the next day when Hylle's men brought in a wagon. They did not stay at the hall but moved on to that upper part of the Dale, to camp at the rock slide. Hylle suggested that the Dalesfolk keep away from the site since the power he would unleash might spring beyond his control.

He allowed Gyrerd, Annet and Ysmay to come nearer than the others. Still they must stand at a distance, watching the hooded men at work among the tumbled rocks. Then, when the leader whistled, all scattered. Hylle, carrying a torch in his hand, touched it to the ground. Having done so, he also ran with great loping strides.

There was a long moment of silence broken only

125

by Hylle's harsh breathing. Then—a roar—a shock— rocks rose in the air, the earth trembled and shook. Stones, split and riven by the thunder, rained down where the men had been a few moments before. Annet held her hands over her ears and screamed. Ysmay stared at the chaos the blast had left. The solid dam of rock was broken, pounded into loose rubble, and already the hooded men were upon it with pick and shovel. Gyrerd spoke to Hylle.

"What demon's work is this, brother?"

Hylle laughed. "No demon obeys me. This is knowledge I have gained through long study. But the secret is mine—and will turn on him who tries it if I am not by."

Gyrerd shook his head. "No man would want to use that. You say it is not demon raised, yet to me it seems so. To each his own secrets."

"Fair enough. And this one will work for us. Could any hand labor so clear our path?"

Twice Hylle used his secret. After the debris of the second blast was cleared, they fronted a cleft which might once have held a stream. Here the hooded men shoveled loose the remaining rocks of the slide.

Hylle went to the fore of that company, coming back with a handful of blue clay. He waved it before them triumphantly.

"This is the resting place of amber. Soon we shall have reward for our labors."

The hooded men continued to dig. Hylle stayed at their camp, not returning to the Hold. So Ysmay alone made the rest of her preparations for the journey north. Hylle had already warned that he must give no more than ten days to the present searching, since they would pass through rough country and winter was coming.

But the yield through the days and nights of labor (for the crew worked by torchlight and seemed not to sleep) was small. If Gyrerd and the others were disappointed, Hylle seemed not. He shrugged and said it was a matter of luck, and of the stars' guidance.

In the end he made a bargain with Gyrerd, which to Ysmay's hidden surprise, seemed overly generous.

For the few lumps taken out of the cutting, he offered in exchange some of his own wares, far to the advantage of the Dalesmen. Gyrerd made only token protest, accepting the trade avidly. Thus, when Hylle's party rode out of Uppsdale, all which had been found was stowed in the saddlebags of Hylle's own mount.

With a promise of return at the first loosing of spring, the party from Quayth turned to the wilderness in the north. This was indeed unknown country. When the Dalesmen had first come to High Hallack, they had clung to the shores, awed and fearful of the back country. Through generations they had spread inward, venturing west and south, but seldom north.

Rumors spoke of strange lands where those who had held this land earlier still lurked—always to the north and west. During the war the High Lords had sought any allies they could raise, and so had treated with the Were-Riders from one of those unknown sections. In the end the Were-Riders had retired again in that direction. Who knew then what lay beyond the next ridge?

Yet Ysmay was less wary than she might have been. Bred in her was a longing for what lay beyond her door, and she looked about her with interest.

For the space of two days they were in tilled land, spending the first night at Moycroft, now a ruin, abandoned during the war for lack of manpower. But by the third day they were well into the unknown—at least unknown to Ysmay's people, though Hylle seemed to have knowledge of it. Ysmay could see no trail markings, save here and there ruts of wagon wheels, made by Hylle's men.

This was a drear land where a bitter wind blew and one wrapped one's cloak tighter and searched in vain for anything to break the awesome emptiness. To Ysmay's reckoning they were going more north than west, angling back toward the sea. She wanted to ask about Quayth, and the land about it, whether they might have neighbors. But Hylle was seldom with her. And when they were in camp he brought out a reading scroll, sometimes running his finger along crabbed lines, shaping words with his lips, but never speaking them aloud. There was a wall about him she could not breach.

She wondered more and more what it would be like to share a hold with a man who did not even talk to her. That warning he had given on their wedding night, and which she had accepted with relief, now appeared to have another aspect. She did not even have a maid-servant, for Hylle had refused to take any woman of the Dales, saying she would be well served and a maid away from her own kind would be ever pining for home.

Thus turned upon her own resources, Ysmay spent much time thinking. Why had Hylle married her? Surely not just for a few lumps of unworked amber! With all that wealth of his own, he had no need for such a pitiful supply. And because the question was one to which she had no answer, she found it disturbing. The unknown provides rich soil for growing fear.

Hylle was not one of the shieldless men who wished to unite with an old family. And what had she to offer him? He had already made it plain that it was not for her body he had taken her.

Now they threaded through woods. Though the bitter wind no longer lashed, there was nothing reassuring about this forest. Their trail, which had to accommodate the wagon, twisted and turned among trees which were tall and old, whose trunks wore feathery lichens in green, rust, white or even blood red. Ysmay disliked the lichen. Underfoot, centuries of leaves had turned to dark muck and gave forth an unpleasant scent when stirred by the hooves of their mounts.

For a day they traveled so, pausing to eat of their provisions, to breathe the horses and rest. Hylle did not set a fast pace, but he kept a steady one. The silence of the forest acted upon them. There was little speech, and when a man voiced words, he sometimes glanced over his shoulder, as if he feared he had been overheard by one not of their party.

The trees thinned, their way sloped up. They camped that night in hills. There followed days which had so much of a sameness that Ysmay lost track of time.

This was no easy passage in the hills. Hylle took time nevertheless to go out each night with a rod of metal which he held to one eye to look upon the stars. He warned them they must make haste for storms were not too far away.

He was right. The first flakes of snow began before dawn. All were roused out in the dark to ride. Now the slope was down again and in that Hylle appeared to take comfort, though he continued to urge them.

Ysmay had lost her sense of direction, for they had turned this way and that. However, by midmorn, there came a wind which carried a new scent. A man-at-arms had been detailed to ride with her (for Hylle accompanied the wagon). She heard him say, "That is a sea wind!"

They came down into a cut between ridges which ran as straight as if it marked an old road. The ridges banked away the wind, though here the snow piled deeper.

Suddenly the path curved and the right-hand ridge fell away, placing the travelers on a ledge. Cliffs glittered with the accumulation of salt crystals. The sea pounded below. Strangest sight of all was a wider section of ledge where the wind had scoured away the snow to clear three great stone chairs, carved from rock certainly not by nature but by intention. Each bore upon its seat a pillow of snow, softening its harsh austerity.

Ysmay recognized another ancient work of the Old Ones. Now she was sure that they were following a road.

Once more the way turned, this time inland. They saw ahead among the rocky cliffs a structure which seemed a part of its stony setting. It arose by wall and tower to dwarf any Dale-hold.

Hylle loomed out of the fine shifting of snow. With the stock of his whip he pointed to the vast pile.

"Quayth, my lady."

She realized with a chill that her new home was one of the ancient remains. And, contrary to all the precautions and beliefs of her own people, she must dwell in a shell alien to her kind. But there was no turning back. She made an effort not to show her unease.

"It is very large, my lord."

"In more ways than one, my lady." His eyes held, searched her face as they had at the first meeting in the merchant's booth—as if fiercely he willed her to reveal the fear which lay within her. But that she would not do. In a moment he spoke again.

"It is one of the ancient places, which the Old Ones had the building of. But time has been kinder to it than to most such. You will find it not lacking in comfort. Ha—let us home!"

Their weary mounts broke into a trot. Soon they passed the overhang of a great, darksome gate into a vast courtyard whose walls had towers set at four corners.

Two of those towers were round. That through which the gate opened was square. The fourth displayed odd sharp angles, unlike any she had seen before.

Though there were faint gleams of light in some of the narrow windows, no one was here to bid them welcome. Troubled, she came stiffly out of the saddle into Hylle's hold, and stumbled through beginning drifts of snow under his guidance to the door at the foot of the nearest round tower. The others scattered through the courtyard in different directions.

Here there was rest from the wind, the heartening blaze of a fire.

To Ysmay's surprise, instead of a thick matting of rushes and dried herbs on the floor, she saw a scattering of mats and rugs of fur stitched together in fanciful patterns, light matched to dark.

These formed roads and pathways across the stone, the main one leading to an island of warm cheer by the hearth. There stood two tall-backed chairs, cushioned with pads of colorful stuff, even having small canopies above to give the final measure of protection against wandering drafts. There was also a table with platters and flagons. Hylle brought Ysmay to the blaze where she loosed her cloak and held her hands thankfully toward the warmth.

A musical note startled her. She turned her head. He had tapped a bell that hung in a carved framework on the table. Soon a figure came down the winding stair which must serve as a spine for the tower.

Not until the newcomer reached the fire could Ysmay make out who it was. Then she caught her lip that she might not utter her instinctive protest.

For this creature, whose head was level with her own shoulder, was that Ninque who had told the gabbled fortune at the very beginning of this change in her life. Only now the seeress did not wear her fancifully embroidered robe, but rather a furred and sleeveless jerkin over an undertunic and skirt of rusty brown. Her head was covered with a close-fitting cap which fastened with a buckle under her flabby chin. She looked even less likely as a bower woman than as a prophetess.

"Greetings, Lord—Lady." Once more that soft voice came as a shock from the obese body. "By good fortune you have outrun the first of the bad storms."

Hylle nodded. When he spoke it was to Ysmay.

"Ninque will serve you, Lady. She is very loyal to my interests." There was an odd emphasis in his words. Ysmay was intent only on the fact that he intended to leave her with this oddling.

She lost pride enough to start to lay her hand in appeal on his arm. But in time she bethought herself and did not complete the gesture. He was already at the outer door before she could summon voice.

"You do not rest—sup—here, my lord?"

There was a glitter in his eyes which warned her. "The master of Quayth has one lodging, and none troubles him in it. You will be safe and well cared for here, my lady." And with that he was gone.

Ysmay watched the door swing shut behind him. Again the dark question filled her mind. Why had he brought her here? What did he need or want of her?

# 4

YSMAY STOOD at a narrow slit of window, looking down into the courtyard. The tracks below made widely separated patterns. In a pile constructed to house a host, there seemed to be a mere handful of indwellers. Yet this was the eve of Midwinter Day. In all the holds of the Dales there would be preparation for feasting. Why should men not rejoice at the shortest day of the frigid winter when tomorrow would mean the slow turn to spring?

However, in Quayth there were no visitors, no such preparations. Nor did Ninque and the two serving wenches (squat and alien as herself) appear to understand what Ysmay meant when she asked what they were to do. Of Hylle she had seen little. She learned that he dwelt in the tower of sharp angles and that not even his men-at-arms—who had their quarters in the gate tower—ventured there, though some of the hooded men came and went.

Now when she looked back at her hopes, to be ruler of the household here, she could have laughed, or rather wept (if stubborn pride would have allowed her) for the wide-eyed girl who hoped she rode to freedom when she left Uppsdale.

Freedom! She was close-pent as a prisoner. Ninque, as far as Ysmay could learn, was the true chatelaine of Quayth. At least Ysmay had had the wit and wariness to go very slow in trying to assume mistress-ship here. She had not had any humiliating refusal of the few orders she had given. She had been careful not to give many, and those for only the simplest matters concerning her own needs.

This was at least a roomy prison, no narrow dungeon cell. On the ground floor was the big room which had seemed a haven of warmth at her first entrance. Above that was this room in which she stood, covering the whole area of the tower, with a circling open stair leading both up and down. Above were two bare chambers, cold and drear, without furnishing or signs of recent usage.

Here in this second chamber there was a bed curtained with hangings on which the needle-worked pictures were so dim and faded by time that she could distinguish little of the patterns, save that here and there the face of a dimmed figure, by some trick of lamp or firelight, would flare into vivid life for an instant or two, startling her.

There was one which appeared to do this more often than the rest. Thinking of it, Ysmay turned from the window, went to that part of the hanging and spread it with one hand while she fingered the face. This time it was dim, features blurred. Yet only a short time ago she had looked up from the hearth and it had given her a start as if a person stood there watching her with brooding earnestness.

She could close her eyes and see it feature for feature—a human face, which was better than some of the others flickering into life there at night. Some had an alien cast as if their human aspect were but a mask, worn above a very different countenance. This one was human, and something about it haunted her. Perhaps her memory played tricks but she remembered a desperate need in its expression.

Which proved how narrow her present life was, that she must make up fancies about old needlecraft! Ysmay wondered whose needles had wrought this and when. She smoothed the length of cloth with her fingertips, feeling the small irregularities of the stitching.

Then her nails caught in something which was no soft embroidery, but a hard lump. She fingered it, unable to detect it by eye, only by touch. It seemed to be within the material. She went for a hand lamp, holding it as close as she dared.

Here was the figure which had intrigued her. It wore a necklace—and this lump was part of the necklace. Inspection showed it concealed within the threads. With the point of her belt bodkin Ysmay picked delicately at the object. It had been so tightly covered by overstitching that the task was a long one. But at last Ysmay could pull out the ends of cut threads, squeeze what they held into her hand. It was smooth— She held it close to the lamp. Amber certainly! Wrought into a device so intricate that it took her some time to see it in detail.

A serpent crawled and turned, coiled and inter-coiled. Its eyes were tiny flecks of butter amber set in the darker shade of its body. The almost invisible scaling on its sides was a masterwork of carving. In spite of inborn repugnance for scaled creatures, Ysmay did not find the stone unpleasant. In fact, the opposite was true.

Then—she gave a little cry and would have flung it from her but she could not.

Those coils were turning, writhing, coming to life!

She watched with horror as the serpent straightened from the involved knot in which she had found it, then coiled again in the hollow of her palm after the fashion of the living kind it resembled. Its head was upheld, with the yellow eyes turned to look at her, and there was a flickering at its tiny mouth as if of tongue play.

For a long moment they remained so, Ysmay and the thing she had freed. Then it slid across her hand while she still could not move to hurl it away. It was not cold as a serpent would have been, but warm. She was aware of light perfume. Certain rare ambers had that scent.

Down to her wrist, under the edge of her sleeve, the serpent went. She felt the warmth encircle her arm and snatched back her sleeve. The serpent was now a bracelet, one she could not rid herself of, no matter how hard she tried. She must either cut it in twain or break it into bits.

Ysmay returned to a chair by the fire, holding her arm stiffly before her. What she had seen was not possible. True amber had once been a part of a living tree. The old idea that it was dragon spittle or dung was only a tale. Living things were found entrapped in it, such as small insects. She recalled the flying thing

Hylle had shown her. But the stuff itself did not live! It had certain odd properties to amuse the curious. Rub it well and it would draw to it, as a magnet attracts iron, small bits of chaff, hair and the like. It could be crushed and distilled into oil.

Distilled! Ysmay stood up, her hand still outstretched lest her wrist touch her body. She went to the chest which she had packed with such care at Uppsdale. She had to use both hands to lift the heavy lid. She searched among the packets.

At last she found what she sought, brought out the bag which could be the answer to any witchery. Back in her chair she worried open the fastening, using her one hand and her teeth.

She savored the good odor from within. Of all herbs grown this was the greatest defense against the powers of dark—angelica, herb of the sun in Leo, talisman against poison and evil magic. Ysmay stretched forth her wrist to expose the serpent. Taking a pinch of the precious herb she rubbed it along the brown-red thread of body.

But the circle remained solid, as it might have been if wrought in this form from the beginning. She rubbed it well and then drew out the amulet of Gunnora. For *She* who was the protector of life would stand against all things of the Shadow. And to the serpent she touched that talisman. Word by word she repeated the charm.

> *Life is breath, life is blood.*
> *By the seed and by the leaf,*
> *By the springtime with its flood,*
> *May this power bring relief!*

She might as well be dealing with any ordinary bracelet. Yet she had witnessed the transformation and knew differently.

Cut it, break it! Even as Ysmay looked about for the means of doing either she saw the fire. Fire! Amber would melt at the touch of fire. She felt now she could endure burns on her flesh rather than carry this band.

But she found she could not reach for a brand. Instead she huddled in the chair, staring at the serpent. Its yellow eyes turned upon her. Larger those eyes grew until at last they merged into one circle of light, and it was as if she looked through a window.

Among shadows and pools of light, she caught glimpses of tables piled with strange bottles, loops of metal, bowls—the sullen glare of a furnace was in evidence. Then she was looking into another chamber cut by pillars.

The contents startled and frightened her. For even as the winged thing had been enclosed in Hylle's cylinder, here other shapes were enclosed, save these were much larger.

Some were so grotesque she gasped, but these were swiftly passed. Ysmay was drawn to the center of the chamber where stood two pillars apart from the others.

In one, the nearer, was a man. His face might be Hylle's save for a subtle difference, as if they were akin in blood but not in spirit. This was less the Hylle of Quayth than the Hylle she had seen at the fair. Looking upon him Ysmay felt again that strange excitement which had first moved her. Also it seemed that his staring eyes sought hers in turn.

But Ysmay no longer faced the man in amber. Now she was drawn to the other pillar and it held a woman.

Her dark hair was dressed high and held in a net of gold. The net was studded with flowers carved of butter amber. She also wore a circlet of dark amber in the form of a serpent. Her robe was silken and amber in color and about her throat was a necklace of nuts, each encased in clear amber. These glowed, seeming to blaze higher when Ysmay looked upon them.

The woman's eyes were open like the man's. While there was no sign of life about her features, those eyes reached Ysmay with appeal so strong it was as if she shouted aloud for aid.

Ysmay felt a whirling of the senses. Images formed in her head and were diffused before she could understand. Only that terrible need, that cry for help, remained. And in that moment she knew that she could not refuse to answer—though what the woman and man wanted from her she could not tell. A picture in her mind, imposed over the pillars as if a veil arose, was the courtyard of Quayth as she could see it from her tower. And what she faced now was the angled tower of Hylle's forbidden domain. She was certain that this chamber of the image lay within its walls.

Then that picture shriveled and was gone. The pillar chamber, too, disappeared. She was blinking at the fire on the hearth.

"Lady—" Ninque's soft voice broke the quiet.

Ysmay hurriedly dragged her sleeve over the serpent, hid Gunnora's amulet in a swiftly closed hand. But nothing could conceal the scent of the angelica.

"What is it, Ninque? I have thought to order my herbs and see if I have the making for a Midwinter Eve cup."

The woman's thick nostrils had widened, testing the air.

"Lord Hylle would speak with you, Lady."

"Then let him do so." As the woman turned her broad back, Ysmay slipped the cord of the amulet back over her head, hiding the talisman. Then she resealed the packet of angelica.

"My lord?" she looked up as Hylle came with his almost silent tread. Even if one could not hear his footfall on the fur mats of the room, one could sense his coming. He was like an invisible force disturbing the air. "It is Midwinter Eve, yet I have heard nothing of any feast." She must play the innocent wrapped in the customs of the life she had left behind.

But she found herself searching his features intently. How much was he like that other? If memory did not deceive her the subtle difference had deepened. Had Hylle of the fair worn a mask now laid aside in Quayth?

"Midwinter Eve," he repeated as if the words were in some foreign tongue. "Oh—a feast of your people. Yes, I am sorry, my lady, but you must keep it alone this year. An urgent message has come to have me ride out. Nor may I return before the morrow's morn." Then he was sniffing the air. "What have you here, my lady? The scent is new to me."

She gestured to the open chest. "Herbs. I have some small skill in their growing and usage, my lord. Now I check my store against the need for savor or scent. But—" she went to place the packet with the others— "since we shall have no feast, I need not concern myself with such."

"I am truly rebuked, my lady, that I have been so apart from you since our homecoming—and that I have not taken heed of the passing of time nor the fact that this feast was near. Forgive me this time and I shall not err again."

Instinct told her that these were merely words and that his feeling for her was such that he believed vague promises would always satisfy her as they might a child.

He went after several more meaningless words of courtesy and she watched from the window as he rode with his men-at-arms. Ninque came in shortly with a bronze bowl. In it was a necklace of many pendants. Their design alternated greenish and bluish amber. She guessed that the piece was a rarity, perhaps worth all the portable goods in the Uppsdale Hold.

Ysmay put the necklace on before a mirror. She simulated pleasure, calling Ninque and the two wenches who came with her supper to see how fine a gift her lord had sent her. She hoped her acting was good enough to deceive Ninque.

She had fastened her sleeve bands tightly at the wrist and there was no chance of the woman spying what she wore there. When Ysmay sat down to eat she filled a horn cup and half raised it to her lips. Then she shook her head.

"I do not speak ill of your brewing," she said lightly. "But were mint added this would be a better drink. Have you ever drunk it so?"

"We know not much of southern herbs in these parts, lady. Our Quayth is in the path of too chill winds to let such grow. Mint I have heard of, but of its use so, that I have not."

"Then you shall taste and tell me whether or no you think I speak the truth. This is a feast eve among my people, Ninque. Since my lord cannot keep it with me, perhaps you will—"

For a moment the woman hesitated. Between her lips the tip of a pale tongue showed for an instant. Then her eyes, those ever-watchful eyes, went to the pitcher on the table.

"There is not enough for a second cup, my lady. You have ever refused more than one, so the wench did not bring it."

"Then have one of them fetch more, Ninque. Do not deny me even this poor revel on a feast eve."

Ninque turned to the stair reluctantly as one who had no excuse for doing otherwise, but would refuse if she could. Ysmay raised her horn again. She could detect in it only the odor of a good brew. But she was as sure as if someone stood at her shoulder speaking a warning, that there was something more in it. Poison? No, that she did not credit. But there were growing things which could be used in cunning ways, to bring deep sleep, to haze the wits so that memory would after play one false.

Why so sharp a suspicion came to her now, she was not to know. She knew only that she was warned. No sooner had Ninque gone than Ysmay was moved to action she did not understand. She unfastened her sleeve, held her bared wrist above the cup.

Instantly the serpent moved, but now its action made her more curious than afraid—even excited her as the prospect of battle might excite a fighting man.

The head of the serpent darted down to dip in the liquid, stirring it. Then it snapped up, once more catching the tip of its tail in its mouth, and hardening into a bracelet.

Ninque came up the stair with a tray on which sat a horn cup which she placed on the table. Ysmay went to her chest. Mint, yes, but she palmed another herb as well, with a skill at concealment she would not have believed herself capable of. While it was mint alone that she sprinkled in her own cup, the mint was mingled with another powder to flavor Ninque's. Then she took up a small spoon to stir each well.

"By rights, Ninque—" she smiled—"being both women, we should have a sprig of ivy to dip in this for luck, then to fling into the fire to take all evil fortune with it. For my lord it would be holly—but ivy is for women. Since we have it not, I bid you good fortune."

"And so I do wish you, Lady," said Ninque.

Ysmay drank, though it was hard with that suspicion within her. How effective had the serpent been to counteract anything wrong—she did not know. But she was convinced that in its way the serpent was her protection, since Gunnora's charm had not repelled it.

"What think you of mint?" She had emptied her cup, set it aside.

Ninque put down her own.

"It has a fresh and pleasing taste, Lady. Your southern growths must be strong. Now—if you will excuse me—I must see to the wenches. You spoke of a feast and my lord was ashamed he had forgotten. But we shall do the best we can for the morrow."

"Which is right courteous. But true to the favor my lord has shown me. Yes, you may go, Ninque. I shall bed early, I think. For some reason I am sleepy."

Was she right in her guess—that the doctored drink was meant to drug her? She could read no change in Ninque's expression.

But after the woman had gone, Ysmay once more loosened her sleeve and held the serpent at eye level. This time it did not open any vision for her.

"I know not what is wanted of me," she addressed the carving in a whisper. "But there are many mysteries in Quayth, and perhaps danger of more than one kind. I cannot draw sword, but neither do I bend my neck to the yoke willingly. Whatever is to be laid upon me, let it begin here and now, for it is better to face danger squarely, than to wait for its coming while courage grows thin."

In the long moment of silence thereafter it came

into her mind what must be done. She arose, put aside her outer garments, and donned her riding skirt which gave her greater freedom of movement. And she took her cloak of gray.

At the head of the stairs she listened and, when there was no sound below, she moved. She had learned that those sections of building uniting the towers were the quarters of the hooded people. With any luck Ninque and the wenches were safely back in their own.

Ysmay had to use both hands to draw open the outer door. The quickest way to the angled tower was straight across the courtyard. But she had no mind to reveal her going to any at some window.

Instead she slipped along the wall, her cloak and skirt dragging in the drifted snow until she reached the door to Hylle's stronghold. The hand she raised to its latch was the one above the serpent.

There was no lock. The door swung easily, perhaps too easily, to her pull.

# 5

A ROOM OF sharp angles was but dimly lighted. Ysmay gasped, for facing her was a cloaked figure. Then she raised her serpent-girdled arm, and that other copied her gesture. She realized she fronted a mirror.

But for the mirror and two lamps high in wall niches, there was nothing—save smell. Her nose tingled at the war of strange odors here. Some might have been pleasing, but they were nigh overcome by acrid whiffs she could not identify.

She turned slowly, peering into those dusky angles. By her survey she discovered what could not be seen from the courtyard, that this tower had been erected in the form of a five-pointed star. She had a vague recollection of ancient lore concerning such a star.

However it was not this bare, shadowed room she sought. Seeing a stairway within one of the angles, she ascended. The steps were worn in depressions, as if from long use. In fact the whole interior of this tower carried the weight of years in its stones, as if a toll of centuries had settled upon it.

Thus Ysmay came into a chamber crowded with such a wealth of things as she could not sort into any understandable array. There were tables filled with curls of metal piping, with retorts, with bottles and flagons —some of which she recognized as akin to those used in herb distilling. And there were things she could not name at all.

She feared to touch anything. For that mingling of odors was very great, almost overpowering, bringing more than a hint of danger. Ysmay rubbed her fingers across the serpent.

For some reason it was lighter here, enough to show still another stair. Ysmay took care in crossing to it, threading a way by those littered tables, holding tight her cloak lest she brush something from one of them.

So she came up to the room of her vision. Here were the pillars forming first an outer star, and then an inner. Against the far wall were two tables. At the point of each star row were candlesticks as high as her own shoulder. In each burned a candle wrist thick. The flames were not honest red-gold, but bluish, making her own flesh look unhealthy and diseased.

Her hand went forth of its own accord. Someone might have held a chain fastened to her wrist, jerked it without warning, to draw her. She walked between two of the outer pillars, coming so to the center.

Before her was the woman of her vision, and the man who was Hylle, yet not Hylle. Imprisoned though they were, their eyes lived, fastened avidly on her as if they strove to cry aloud what must be done. Yet if they had had the power to bring her here, that power was limited, for no message reached her.

But she could not doubt what they wanted—their freedom. Could people be so encased and yet live? This was magic such as she had met only in old legends.

"What must I do?" she begged them. She touched the surface of the pillar which encased the woman. To her fingers it was solid. Broken? Cut? Amber was

a soft material, easily worked. A knife might chip away
its substance.

Ysmay drew her belt knife, used the point in a hack-
ing blow, only to have good steel rebound as if she
had struck at a stone. The force jarred her arm. Not
even a scratch was left on the surface of the pillar.

That there was a way to free them she did not
doubt, but it must lie in magic. She stepped away and
turned slowly around, surveying the whole group of
pillars set star within star. The blue light made even
more fantastic the grotesque heads and bodies. But she
forced herself to a full inspection.

Those of the outer star were not human, but a mixture of weird forms. The second star held more humanoid figures, half of them small, squat, wearing tu-
nics like men.

Their bodies were thick, wide of shoulder, arms long,
out of proportion. From their fingers and toes pro-
truded long curved claws, closer to the talons of some
bird or animal than to a human nail. Their faces—these
surely had kinship with Ninque's people.

Nails, squat shapes—Ysmay fitted what she saw to
make a thought which brought a shiver to her. The
hooded men with their gloves—Hylle's followers who
kept, or were kept, apart from the Dalespeople. Was
this their real appearance? But why were these few
pillar-bound?

It was a relief to look back to the wholly human
forms of the man and woman. Once more their eyes
burned, besought— If she could only understand what
she could do—must do!

Those eyes were closing! There was a shade of in-
tense concentration on their faces. Impulsively Ysmay
raised her hand, shook back her sleeve so that the serpent was free. Because once before she had looked
into its eyes with strange results, she did so again.

Larger—larger—now she stared at a single yellow globe,
clean, free from the blue taint of the others. This time
no window formed through which she viewed another
place. Rather there was a whispering voice. Because
she sensed that what it would tell her was of utmost

importance, she strained to catch words, to make coherence of the sound. But there was no intelligible message. And at last the whisper died away.

She swayed. Her back and her feet ached, as did her head. She might not only have stood in that position for a length of time, but she felt as if she had concentrated on some mental exercise too hard for her. Ysmay sighed and let her stiff arm fall to her side.

The eyes of those in the pillars were open, but they were dull, dimmed. No longer was there that spark of vigorous demand. Whatever they had tried had failed.

Still she could not leave them. The knife had failed, and communication. With some vague hope of finding assistance, she made her way among the pillars to those tables she had sighted at her entrance.

They did not bear such utensils as she had seen below. But still—at least on one table—she did not like what she saw.

On it stood a cup. The foot was amber, dark, cracked, worn and warped. Its bowl was of a gray-white material. The interior was stained. Beside it, naked point to the stars, was a knife, its hilt the gray of the bowl, its blade— Ysmay jerked away, for along the blade crawled and writhed lines of red, as if runes of some forbidden knowledge formed, vanished, ran again.

There was a book, laid open at midpoint. Its pages were yellowed, wrinkled, inscribed with heavy black lines of writing unlike any she had seen before. There was one ornamented capital on each page, but not wreathed by flowers like those in old chronicles. No, here were two small scenes which brought a flush of shame to her face as she looked upon them, so vile were they, yet so ably done that they lingered hatefully in the mind.

Here also was an upright frame in which hung a bell of discolored metal, and beside it the mallet which would make it sound. Last of all was a candle-holder so wrought that once more she flushed. The candle it held was misshapen, beginning as one thick piece and then subdividing into five thinner portions of unequal length.

Evil hung so strongly here Ysmay could believe it visible as a black cloud. She backed away, thus coming to the second board. What lay there was different— irregular lumps of amber new taken from bedding. She thought she could even recognize those which had been passed from hand to hand at Uppsdale. There were few enough of them, very small showing compared with the wealth in those pillars.

The evil things, which Ysmay did not doubt were used for black ensorcelment, the rough amber— She had seen enough to guess that Hylle wrought ill here. And she was oath-tied to him!

Black indeed were the tales she had heard. There were men reported to have dealings with the older powers rooted here. Was Quayth a garden that brought forth evil harvest?

On impulse Ysmay drew forth the amulet of Gunnora. The old shadowed ways were those which dealt with death and destruction, but Gunnora stood for life and light. How much protection lay in her talisman, Ysmay could not guess. But she felt stronger for holding it.

A table of amber lumps, another which was a shrine to vile powers, and the prisoners in the pillars. Also— when Hylle returned what would be her fate? She tried to think clearly and to some purpose.

This was a fateful night, one of the four within the year when certain powers were loosed for good or ill. Hylle had fared forth. What did he seek out in the cold and the night? Some greater force than any he could raise within these walls?

Ysmay turned once more to look upon the double star of the pillars, the blue burning candles. Power was locked herein. Why had she been able to pass freely through any safeguard Hylle must have set? For such places had their guards which humankind dared not meddle with.

Was it a trap, and she had been allowed to walk in? That she must test! Gripping Gunnora's amulet, Ysmay hurried for the stairs, turning her face from the two in the pillars as she passed. Down she went without hindrance into the ground floor chamber—

Only to stop in fear. For the mirror on the wall reflected another form. It stood unmoving, neither advancing to cut her off from the door, nor to seize her.

Horrible it was, but now she could see it was no creature living, but rather a tall carving of amber, wrought into demon form. Whence had it come? Who had brought it here?

She sped past it to the door, gave a great push. To her vast relief the door swung open readily and the fresh cold air of night was like freedom itself.

Once more she rounded the walls and gained her own tower. She slipped inside breathing quickly, looking for Ninque or one of the wenches.

Empty—the coals on the hearth gave enough light to make sure. Ysmay scuttled for the stairs, won to her bedchamber, crossed to the window to look out. Had any tracked her from the star tower? If so, they had left no footprints in the snow that was now being whirled about by a rising wind. With luck its shifting would cover her path.

She sat down on the bed and tried to make sense of all she had seen. Hylle had told her he was both astrologer and alchemist. The second chamber of the star tower, with all that clutter of equipment, could be the work place of an alchemist. Such learning was in the bonds of reason, though few of the Dalesmen had it.

But the top chamber was different. Ysmay rubbed her hands across her eyes, remembering far too well that which lay on the first table—the foul book, all the rest. What was done there was not the result of straightforward learning.

As for the prisoners in the pillars, most had shown no signs of life. But she had not lingered to examine them closely. However, she was sure that the man and the woman were held in some foul ensorcelment. She must think—if Hylle had the power to do that, what chance had she against him?

She could creep out of Quayth perhaps this night.

Creep—to die of cold and exposure in the wilds. She had no chance without supplies or plan to survive the long journey back to the Dales. Sure death one way— but to stay might mean worse than death. She must chance that.

Ysmay laid aside her cloak, undressed, putting her garments back in a chest so Ninque might not remark them later. Then she crawled into bed, drawing tight the curtains, so that she lay in a darkness which for that moment felt safe. But the serpent was still on her wrist. And around her neck Gunnora's charm.

Perhaps she slept. Afterward she could not remember. Then, as if someone had summoned her, she sat up. The dark was gone. Instead there was dim twilight within the tent of the curtains. Somehow she was able to see the pictures there.

Ysmay had thought their patterning had been given only on the outer side, facing the room. But here they glowed, as if their half-lost outlines were drawn in the cold, clear light of starshine. They were of many kinds, but notable among them was a face. The woman in the pillar!

To her great surprise and fear, the lips writhed on the face, as if a portrait worked with needle and thread fought for speech. And Ysmay heard a small sound, like a gasp for breath.

"The serpent—key—key—"

The light faded, she could no longer see the face as she sat hunched among the tumbled coverings. The serpent was warm about her wrist, as if lit by an inner fire.

"Key—" Ysmay repeated aloud. Key to what? To be found where? She pulled at the curtain—should she return to the star tower? There was light in the chamber, but it came from the dawn. Her chance was gone. If she would make another invasion of Hylle's place she must wait for nightfall.

The day was long and through it she played a taxing role. Ninque brought forth feast dainties and also stayed within call. While Ysmay busied her brain with planning. She dared not try once more to drug Ninque's cup, for she did not underestimate the woman, and to issue another such invitation might awake her suspicions. Was her usual attentiveness today a sign that she was watching Ysmay for some purpose?

Her plans came to nothing because at dusk Hylle and his men rode in. She watched them from the window, steeling herself against the need of fronting the dark lord without revealing any unease.

To her relief he did not come directly to her, but went to the star tower. Then her relief was quickly gone as she wondered if her intrusion had left some trace. That thing of amber before the mirror—whoever had transported it there could well have seen her.

Ysmay twisted her hands together, her fingers seeking the serpent band. A key—to what? She was like one who had an invisible sword lying to hand yet could not find it for her defense.

She drew on her powers of self-control. To seem as usual she must work hard. She went down to the lower chamber where Ninque was setting out the evening meal.

"My lord has returned." Ysmay was surprised at the steadiness of her voice.

Ninque looked up. "It is so. Do you wish to bid him to your table, my lady?"

Ysmay nodded. "This is a feast night. If he is not tired from his journeying, perhaps he will find some small pleasure so. Can you send a message—"

"I, myself, will go, my lady. He will wish to share your feast." There was almost a note of authority in that, as if Ninque could urge this on her master and be obeyed.

Ysmay stood by the fire, facing the door, summoning strength against this meeting. Hylle had been strange enough, a person to evoke awe before. But now—now that she suspected what he might do, could she face him showing no measure of what she had learned?

It seemed long, that wait until Ninque returned. The woman, not shedding her cloak, said in her usual soft and insinuating voice, "My lady, my lord has prepared a feast for your tasting. He would have you come—"

Ninque did not finish her sentence. For Hylle entered. There was a light powdering of snow on his cloak and he carried over his arm another drapery of silken material, the color of rich amber. This he shook out to display a cloak with clasps of amber at throat and waist.

"A fairing for my lady." He whipped it about Ysmay before she could move. "And a feast waiting, so come, let us be merry after the custom of your own people."

She could not avoid his grasp, he used the cloak as a net to entrap her. But fear was a cold thrust through her, a sour taste in her mouth. She had wondered why he wanted her, now she was about to learn and she had no defense against him.

Yet he spoke lightly as he drew her with him across the courtyard. They might have been truly man and wife on their way to a happy hour. She dared not reveal her fear lest it weaken her past all hopes of trying to save herself from whatever he planned.

They came into the room of the mirror. There was more light there now, but that monster carving was still in place, only now it faced them at the door.

Hylle's arm tightened about her. Had she betrayed herself with a start? Or could her reaction be counted normal at facing such ugliness?

Still keeping one arm firmly about her waist, Hylle put forth his other hand. The thing moved, stretched upward as might a cat to meet some caress, until his fingers rested upon its spiked crest. But—it must be a carving—not a living thing!

Ysmay heard Hylle's soft laughter. "Does this frighten you, my lady? Did I not warn you I was learned in strange ways. And now you will see that I have strange servants also. But I do not loose this one yet, it shall play sentry for us. Come!"

She fought her fear. That he meant her very ill she was now sure. Yet she had come from generations of fighting men who held their lands against many perils, or fought until death trying to do so.

Under the edge of the cloak he used to engulf and hold her, she caught at the serpent. A key—to what? However she schooled herself against vain hope as they went up and up, past the room which was a work place, into the chamber of pillars. And he pushed her before him, saying:

"Welcome, my lady, to the heart of Quayth. Its secrets you have sought by stealth, now you shall find them out. Though whether you shall relish your enlightenment is another question."

On he urged her between the pillars to the center, then dragged her around to face the two there.

# 6

"You CALL YOURSELF Lady of Quayth, Ysmay of the Dales. Look you now upon the true lady of this hold, Yaal the Far-Thoughted. I wonder where her thoughts now range, since she can travel by thought alone. Wench, she is such as your upstart blood cannot equal. Her rule was old before your people arose from root-grubbing savages."

He looked upon Yaal as if he hated yet respected her, with more emotion than Ysmay had seen in him before.

"Yaal—she is such as cannot be dreamed of by your ignorant breed. Just as Quayth, Quayth was once what it shall be again—since I have the will and now the tools to make it so.

"You gave me those, wench, for which thank that small power you bow head to. Otherwise—you would be as a flea cracked between the nails and dropped into the fire. For you brought me the seed from which I shall grow much. Hear that, my Lady Yaal? Did you dream that I had come to the end of my power when my supply of amber was finished? If you did you underestimated me and the greed of these Dale barbarians!

"I have amber again. Yes, and many strange uses for it. Hear you that, Yaal!" And he held out his hand as if to tap on the surface of the pillar, but did not quite touch it.

Yaal's eyes were open but the girl could read no message, not even a spark of life in them. Hylle's grip loosened. Impulsively Ysmay shook back the hampering folds of the cloak, made a deep reverence to the prisoner.

Hylle stared. "What do you, wench?"

"Did you not say she is lady here, my lord?" Ysmay did not know what moved her, it was as if action and words were dictated by another. "Then it is meet that I pay her honor. And he—" she turned her head to nod at the other pillar—"if she be lady, is he lord here?"

Hylle's face was convulsed. He struck out at her viciously and she could not dodge the full force of the blow. It sent her spinning against the pillar which held the man and she clung to it to keep her feet.

In Hylle's hand there was now a glittering, golden rope. He swung it loopwise as he mouthed words which had no meaning for Ysmay. The loop whirled, circled about her, fell to the floor. Then Hylle's face was smooth, guarded. He had regained control.

"Bide my pleasure here, wench. It will be for a long time. I go to prepare the means to assure that now."

He left, and Ysmay was bewildered. That shining circle, now that she had time to examine it, was composed of beads of amber strung on a chain. She could not guess its purpose.

But Hylle was gone, and if the serpent was a key, she must bestir herself to find the lock. She took a step forward, to discover that she could not cross the amber circle. It kept her as tightly prisoner as if she were in a cage.

For a second or two she was as strongly held by fear as by the chain. Then the strength of her breed returned and she forced herself to think rather than feel. It was plain that Hylle controlled great powers. He kept these two captive, which meant that, as his enemies, they were potential allies for her. If she could enlist their aid—

The serpent was the key, but how to use it? Ysmay

looked at the woman, then the man. She stood between them, but closer to the man. Moistening her lips with her tongue, she thought of keys and locks—

There was no visible lock, but then neither was the serpent an ordinary key. Locks—the pillar people were locked— She shook back her sleeve, reached out her arm until she could touch the serpent head to the amber casing about the man.

Around her wrist was a blaze of fire which brought a small, choked cry from her. But she held it fast.

The amber pillar began to change. From that small point of contact it filmed, darkened to an ashy dullness. Cracks appeared in it, ran in jagged lines, widened to fall in flakes. And the flakes on the floor powdered into dust.

A tremor ran through the newly freed prisoner. She saw his chest expand as he drew in a great breath. His hands arose in small, jerky movements to his head, slipped down over cheeks and chin as if he sought thus to assure himself of his own being.

He did not look at her but rather stepped stiffly from the pillar base and stood, his head turning from side to side, as if he sought something which should be in plain view and yet was not.

If he hunted some weapon, he was not to have time for a thorough search.

From the stairhead came a rasping hiss. Ysmay cried out. The monster thing from the lower chamber hunched there, its hideous head darting as might a snake's seeking to strike.

The man faced it with empty hands and Ysmay thought he had little chance if the thing rushed him. Yet he raised those hands and, using his two pointing forefingers, he sketched in the air.

Glowing lines of light appeared, a grill of them crossing and recrossing. Behind that strange barrier, he put a partly clenched fist to his lips as if he held a trumpet, and loosed a murmur of sound.

Ysmay could distinguish no words, only low crooning notes repeated over and over. The monster paced back and forth, its armored tail twitching in frustration, the spines on its head erect. It edged among the pillars, but kept a wary distance from the light. And still the man crooned those three notes over and over again.

Then—

From out of the air swooped a bolt of blue fire, the ugly color of the candles. Seemingly heartened, the monster, too, surged forward, shaking its head from side to side as if it advanced under a rain of blows.

The man showed no dismay. The sound of his murmuring voice grew stronger. There was more movement in the chamber, beyond the candles, someone sliding along the wall.

Ysmay, without seeing the pale face of that newcomer, still knew it was Hylle. He was trying to reach not the freed captive but—

The table! That table where lay the instruments of black sorcery. And it would seem that his former captive had not yet sighted him.

Ysmay would have cried aloud in warning, but she found that she could not. It might have been the power of the ring about her feet which also stifled the voice in her throat. Yet she had been able to use the serpent once—what else might she do with it?

She stretched forth her arm at an awkward angle so that she might touch the yellow-eyed head to the circlet about her. There was a flare of blue fire. She cried out, using her hands to shield her face from the fierce glow. There appeared to be no heat in the flames, only blinding light.

The flash seemed to dim her sight. Tears ran down her cheeks as she fought to see, though it was like peering through a thick veil. She could not make out even the shadow of Hylle.

She felt about her and touched the smooth surface of that other pillar. If the serpent had freed the man, why not Yaal? She laid the wristlet to the casing of amber.

This time Ysmay could not see the result, but she could feel the cracking, the crumbling. And the dust of it sprinkled her hands, puffed about her body. There was movement. Hands caught her, pulled her erect,

153

steadied her for an instant against a firm body. Then both body and hands were gone.

Ysmay wiped her eyes, blinked. Yaal was moving purposefully toward the table. Ysmay stumbled in her wake. Her eyes were clearing. She could see.

The assault of blue flames continued. The monster was now within the first row of pillars, weaving back and forth, a wild slaver dripping from its jaws. Ysmay's hand tightened around Gunnora's amulet.

Yaal reached the table, but Hylle was there, too. They fronted each other. His face was a mask of hate and malice, his lips flattened against his teeth as if he would show the same poisonous fangs the monster bore.

His hand flashed out, finger closing about the hilt of the knife. He flicked the keen blade across his own palm, tried to spill the quickly welling blood into the encrusted cup. But Yaal raised her finger and pointed, and straightaway the cut was closed into a seam of an old scar. No blood, save for a drop or two, entered the bowl.

"Not so, Hylle." Her voice was low, but it carried above the hissing of the monster and the crooning that kept it at bay. "Not even with *your* blood can you summon—"

"Tell me not what I may do!" he cried. "I am Hylle, Master—"

Yaal shook her head. "Only because of our lack of caution did you become Master. Your day is done, Hylle."

She did not turn her head to look to Ysmay, but she held out her right hand.

"Let the serpent come," she ordered.

Ysmay, as if she understood perfectly what was to be done, raised her own hand. She felt the circlet come alive. It streaked across her flesh to leap through the air, fall into Yaal's palm, move so swiftly that it was a blur, to encircle Yaal's wrist.

Hylle started forward as if to prevent the transfer. But he was too late.

"Now." Yaal held up her hand. The serpent, though

in a hoop, was not inert. Its head swayed and its eyes glowed with yellow fire.

*Aphar and Stolla, Worum, awake!*
*What was once drunk, must be tongued.*
*What was wrought, you must unmake!*
*In the Name of—*

But that final word was no name, only a roaring and a tumult in the room, which made Ysmay cry out and cover her tormented ears.

The cup on the table began to whirl in a mad dance. Hylle, with a cry, tried to catch it. The knife fell from his grasp and leaped into the air, where it dangled enticingly as he strove to lay hand upon it, seeming to forget all else.

It bobbed and dangled, always just a fraction beyond his reach. As he scrambled after it Ysmay saw there were no longer any flashes of blue fire, and that the crooning sounds had a note of triumph.

The flying goblet brought Hylle well away from the table, close to where those shattered pillars had stood. Then he seemed to awake from whatever spell had held him. He whirled about, crouched like a swordsman about to leap at an enemy.

"No!" he cried out defiantly. He threw out an arm as if to brush aside the cup and came soft-footed, with so deadly a look that Ysmay shrank back, toward the two tables. This time he did not try to reach those instruments of evil. Instead his hands clutched at the lumps of unworked amber.

"Yet—yet—" he screamed. Holding the amber, he ran for the stairs. None tried to stop him. Instead Yaal went to the table of evil. There stood the cup as if it had never risen. The knife lay beside it.

Yaal gazed, her serpent-girdled hand extended. The head of the creature still swayed from side to side. It was as if she now memorized something of vast importance. Then, as if she had come to a decision, she turned again.

There was less sound. Ysmay looked around. The

grille of light was dimming. And the monster had withdrawn, snuffling and hissing, to the head of the stair. Yaal joined her fellow prisoner.

"Let be. His mind is closed. There can be only one end, as we should have known long ago."

He dropped his hand from his lips and nodded. "He made the choice, abide by it now he shall!"

But Yaal wore a look of faint perplexity. She glanced right and then left.

"There is something else," she said slowly. "Do you not feel it, Broc?"

He lifted his head as if to a wind and his nostrils expanded to breathe the air.

"It is she!" For the first time he looked at Ysmay as if she were a presence.

Now Yaal eyed her also.

"She is no creature of his, she has worn the serpent. This is another power. Hylle deals in death, or life-in-death. This is a power of life. What charm do you hold, girl?"

Ysmay answered by holding out her hand so that Gunnora's amulet might be seen. Yaal studied it for a moment and then nodded.

"It has been long and long again since that device has been seen at Quayth. The protection of Rathonna—Yes, to add to what he had, Hylle would want that indeed."

The girl found her tongue. "But he did not take it from me when he could have."

Yaal shook her head. "Such a thing of power must come only as a gift. Taken by force it will turn against its user. One does not deal lightly with Rathonna."

"I do not know the name. This is an amulet of Gunnora."

"What is a name?" Yaal asked. "Certain powers have always been known and given different names by different peoples. I recognize that as coming from Rathonna. Of old she did not turn her face from us, but was willing to lend her aid when the need arose. If Hylle thought to use *Her*—"

Broc interrupted. "You know Hylle, he would think

156

himself above any threat of reprisal, or else scheme how he could turn it to his own advantage. As he schemes now. Yaal—as he schemes now!"

"The stars have come full turn, and the serpent is ready to strike. I do not think Hylle either schemes nor stirs his great pot to any purpose this night. Now is the hour for us to make an end."

Together they walked toward the stairhead, Ysmay trailing them. She would not stay alone in this haunted place.

The monster hissed. It had flattened its body to the floor and its red eyes were fixed on them. Broc made a pass of hand through the air and between his fingers he now held a sword.

No light reflected from any steel. The blade had no cutting edge, but was ruddy brown and carved as if from wood. However, seeing it, the monster slunk away. It hissed and spat, retreating steadily. Thus they came down to Hylle's workshop, where noxious fumes were heavy.

In the center was a fire in a stone-lined pit. From a crossbar over the fire hung a giant pot into which Hylle was flinging handfuls of objects from a nearby bench. As he filled the pot so he chanted, paying no attention to those who came.

"Are his wits turned?" Broc asked. "Surely he must know that this will not work again."

"Oh, but it will!" Yaal held up her arm. The yellow eyes of the snake glowed, grew larger, larger, became a single orb, a sun hanging in the dark room. The monster gave a bubbling scream.

It raced across the floor—not toward the three by the stair, but for its master. At the same time the amulet flamed in Ysmay's hand. The color it gave off was green, and its light rippled and lapped across the floor, speeding to the pit.

The green flood boiled over the lip but did not douse the flames, merely set them leaping higher. Now they were green flames.

Ysmay heard the break in Hylle's chant. He screamed as the monster reached him. They writhed together, tottered and fell forward, still entwined, into the bubbling pot.

Instantly the orb was gone, the green flames died. In the pot a liquid seethed quietly just below the rim, and there was no way of seeing below the surface.

Dawn and a new day. Ysmay leaned against the outer wall of the star tower. It was hard to believe that she could breathe the fresh winter air after the fumes of the tower and its stench of evil. That she had survived the night past was a miracle. For the moment she was content with that alone.

Then Yaal's hand was on her arm and they were three in the courtyard with the gray sky above them.

"It is changed, sad changed," Yaal said. "This is not Quayth as it should be."

"It can be changed again," Broc said briskly. "That which ate its heart is gone. And we have the future—"

What of Ysmay? She was not Lady of Quayth, nor had ever been. Would she now ride to Uppsdale, even less than she had been before?

"I was Hylle's wife," she said slowly. "It was by my own choice that I came to Quayth—though I knew not what he was—yet I took this path without protest."

"And so were the saving of us all." Broc looked at her. His face with its resemblance to Hylle moved her in a way she did not understand. No—he was not Hylle, rather what an untried girl once thought Hylle might be. "Nor were you Hylle's wife," he continued, "nor his creature—if you had been, you could not have worn the serpent, or stood with us this night."

"Say not Hylle's wife, but rather Rathonna's daughter!" Yaal's voice had almost the tone of an order. "Many and strange are the weavings of fortune. We are of an old people, we of Quayth, and we have learning which has given us powers the ignorant grant to godlings. Yet we are also of human kind in many ways. That is why we can have such as Hylle among us. They are of our own brood. Hylle wanted to master certain powers it was not right to meddle with—"

"He wanted more," Broc broke in. "He wanted—"

"Me? Perhaps, but rather he wanted what he thought he could gain through me. And he was strong, too strong then, for us, though we did what we could—"

"Like hiding the serpent?" Ysmay asked.

"Like that. But the waiting was long until one would come who could use it, Rathonna's daughter. You say you are not Lady of Quayth, but do not say that again! Hylle wished to use you to gain the true amber he must have to build the false he used for dark purposes. For the false must always have a grain of the true within it. He wished to use you, but you were not for him. Be proud and glad, daughter of Rathonna."

"Welcome to Quayth," Broc added. "And this time a true welcome, doubt not that!"

Nor did Ysmay then, or ever. Though whether she was the Ysmay of Uppsdale in those after days, or someone much changed by fate, she sometimes wondered. Not that it mattered for Quayth's welcome was warm enough to content her.

Nor did she need to go into that shunned tower and look upon a lump of miswrought amber in which man and monster stood locked in endless embrace, to remind herself of what lay behind.

✓

9812